HARBOR TIDES

HARBOR TIDES

A GREY'S HARBOR STORY

LARK GRIFFING

WIND LARK
PUBLISHING

GREY'S HARBOR SERIES

GREY'S LANDING
A Grey's Harbor Story
by Lark Griffing

GREY'S HARBOR
A Grey's Harbor Anthology
By Carol Cassada
Lark Griffing
Piper Malone
Jennifer Sivec
J.C. Wing

HOPE ADRIFT
A Grey's Harbor Story
By Lark Griffing

HARBOR TIDES
A Grey's Harbor Story
By Lark Griffing

Coming Soon ~

HARBOR SONG
A Grey's Harbor Story
By J.C. Wing

PERFECT SEAS
A Grey's Harbor Story
By Jennifer Sivec

This is a work of fiction. Names, characters, organizations, places, events, and incidents are either products of the author's imagination or are used fictitiously

ISBN-13: 978-0-9988719-8-1

Edited by Wing Family Editing

Cover Design by Wicked Whale Publishing

1

"Maeve, I'm sorry, but I'm just not ready." Tank moved to draw Maeve into his muscle-bound arms, but she stiffened and took a step back. Seagulls wheeled above them, and the wind whistled past the old lighthouse sounding like a ghost woman crying in grief.

"I don't think you'll ever be ready, Tank. I'm sorry. I love you with all my heart, but I can't keep waiting, hoping that you'll someday decide we belong together forever." She turned her face away, not wanting him to see the tears glistening in her eyes.

"It's because you want a family, right?" He reached for her again, lifting her chin with his finger so she would look him in the eyes.

"No, well, yes. Damn it, Tank. I'm not that young anymore, and I guess my clock is ticking, but that's not the reason I want us to make this relationship permanent..." She stepped away again and kicked a piece of driftwood, frustrated with having to explain. "I want commitment. I want security. Is that really too much to ask? And if you won't or can't give it, then I understand. It's just not who you are, but Tank, this is not who I am. I can't keep going on like this. I'm sorry, but I have to end it. For me." She looked at him, the misery she was feeling written all over her. Her blonde hair covered her face, partially because the wind blew it there, partially because she wanted to screen herself from him. Protect herself from the man she loved.

"Maeve, I love you," Tank groaned, angry at himself, angry at Maeve, angry with the world.

"I love you, too, Tank, but I'm not going to waste my life waiting for a man who won't commit to loving me forever." With tears streaming down her face, she stretched onto her tiptoes and kissed the man. She loved him, but it would be the last time, she told herself. She was done.

Tank stood stock still. Shocked as he watched the beautiful lady walk away. She bent over, sliding her sandals off her tanned feet and walked toward the surf. The tide was coming in and the waves beat a steady rhythm against the shore. Maeve moved into the water, holding her sandals in her hand, letting the waves rock her body as they hit her calves.

She walked. Away from Tank.

And he let her.

"Hey, sis." Ryker walked across the diner and wrapped his sister in his arms, giving her a bear hug. Her blonde head disappeared in his arms as he pulled her against his chest. "Rough couple of days, huh?" he asked, whispering against her hair so the diners couldn't overhear.

It was a silly attempt at privacy. Everyone in Grey's Harbor knew that Maeve Wynn and Tank Harmond had broken up. Maeve looked up into the deep green eyes that matched her own and smiled.

"I'm hanging in there. Thanks for checking on me, or did you just stop in because you know it's meatloaf night and you adore my meatloaf?"

"I could never lie to you, sis. It's the meatloaf that brought me here."

Maeve swatted her brother and led him to a booth.

"You have lied to me plenty of times and don't forget it, but I forgive you the sins of your youth. Meatloaf, mashed potatoes and gravy? Salad or broccoli?"

"Seriously, Maeve. You know damn well I don't want broccoli. Oh, and extra ranch with that, please."

"Of course. Malt?"

"Not tonight. I would feel guilty having a malt without Jenny."

"Where is she tonight?" Maeve asked, not used to seeing her brother without Jennifer Creely by his side.

"She's over at Cadigan's Marina. There are some more problems with the books. She's with Bridger trying to figure out what's what."

"I thought she took over the accounting for the marina. What happened?"

"She did, but Bridger's mom decided to help out again. No one realized she 'helped', and now there's a mess to clean up." Ryker shook his head sadly.

"Poor Emmeline. She was such an efficient person. Dementia sucks."

"Yes, it does. Bridger needs to make some decisions, but he keeps putting it off. I don't blame him. It has to be hard."

Maeve put a hand on her brother's shoulder. She knew he was hurting for his best friend. She went into the kitchen and came back out with a large salad and two ranch containers. She delivered them to her brother and went back into the kitchen. A few minutes later, she placed the early evening special, her bacon-wrapped grilled meatloaf slices and creamy mashed potatoes, in front of him. She'd been careful to make a deep well in them and poured on the brown gravy, just like her brother liked.

"Thanks. Maeve, if you need to talk. I'm here for you. Hell, I'm here for both of you. Tank is sulking around work, pissed off, and no fun to be around. For the tough guy he is, he sure is a baby." He was hoping he would get a smile from his sister. It didn't work.

"Is he okay?" she asked softly, her eyes misting.

"No, he's not, and neither are you. Can't you guys work it out?"

"I don't think so, Ryker. It's over. I need to move on."

"But you two are meant for each other."

"Ryker, if we were meant for each other, he would've put a ring on my finger. You've said it a million times. You told him to make an honest woman of your sister. The writing's on the wall. Now eat that before it gets cold and let me get back to work. I'm getting ready to close."

She bent down and planted a kiss on her brother's forehead, then hurried away so he wouldn't see her cry.

2

*M*aeve locked the front door to the diner. She was tired. She was used to long hours on her feet, and she loved running the diner. That's not what made her tired. She was just weary from sadness. She didn't remember a time when she had ever felt so alone. She moved down the sidewalk oblivious to the silky summer air that touched her skin, the ocean salt leaving its mark. Normally she would savor a night like this, but not tonight. Tonight, she was pulled inward, her thoughts on Tank and the wounded look in his eyes when she had convinced him it was over.

"Head's up."

Two hands reached out and caught Maeve just before she plowed into the man who had stepped up onto the sidewalk.

"Oh, I'm so sorry," Maeve stammered, still not looking at the man's face but checking her feet which had tangled up on themselves. Those hands were stopping her from hitting the dirt.

"No problem, Maeve. Preoccupied tonight?"

"A little. Oh, Jeff, hi. Thanks. I'm sorry."

He tilted his head and looked the leggy blonde over. She looked good, as always, but her normally easy going face was lined with something…worry, regret?

"No reason to apologize. Forgive me for saying this, but you look like you could use a friend, Maeve." He smiled at her and his eyes crinkled at the corners.

"Ha, it shows, huh?" Maeve looked up at Jeff and decided that he was being sincere. She didn't know him well. He had moved to town a couple of years ago when Jones and Johnson Architects had lost an associate. He filled the bill and seemed to assimilate into Grey's Harbor fairly well. He had been to the diner on many occasions and had made a nice donation to the Oyster Festival fund each year. He seemed like an easy going kind of guy, but he moved in a different crowd and they didn't cross paths often.

"I was going to have some dinner, but I didn't realize it was so late. The diner is closed, I see." Jeff mused as he reassessed his plans.

"I'm sorry. We closed an hour ago. I decided a long time ago that I wasn't interested in the late evening crowd. Early morning breakfast and early dinner and I'm done," she said with an apologetic smile.

"Does this mean that you've already eaten your early dinner?" Jeff asked, his eyebrow cocked, his deep brown eyes searching her face.

"No, I didn't manage to do that tonight," Maeve admitted. Much to her embarrassment, her stomach announced its hunger pangs. Jeff laughed, and after an embarrassed second, Maeve joined him.

"How about you join me at the Mizzen Mast for a bite to eat? Bar food wasn't what I had in mind, but Izzy does make a good burger. What do you say?" He stepped back a little and waited for her response. He didn't want to make her feel at all pressured. He wasn't that kind of guy. From what he remembered, Maeve dated a very muscular, testosterone filled kind of man, and he didn't want to step on anyone's toes.

"You know what?" she said, a slight smile forming on her lips, "I think I'd like that."

"Do you feel like walking there?"

"Sure, it's a nice night. I'm fine with that." She smiled at him making sure he knew that hoofing it wasn't a problem for her. They turned and fell into step together heading down the sidewalk to the Mizzen Mast.

"*H*ey, Maeve," Izzy called over her shoulder as Maeve stepped into the bar. Izzy nodded at Jeff as he walked in behind her. "Hi, Jeff."

"Hi, Maeve," Jeff said, "Does it matter where we sit?"

"Nope, just find a place, and I'll be with you two in a minute. Ryker, Tank, and Bridger are out on the deck," Izzy said with a meaningful look at Maeve.

"Deck or inside, Maeve?" Jeff asked, oblivious to Izzy's meaning.

"Inside would be nice, if that's okay with you." She wasn't in the mood to chit chat or have to deal with Tank once he saw her with Jeff.

Jeff led her to a table at the back wall where the windows looked out onto the river as it flowed lazily by on its way to the ocean. He pulled out her chair for her, seating her, then sat himself and picked up a menu.

Maeve knew Izzy's menu by heart, so she watched Jeff as he looked through the selections. His soft brown hair was cut neat and short, typical of the business set. Overall, he was a good looking guy. He filled out his white business shirt well, but not like Tank who had trouble getting shirts to fit his extremely muscular build. Her heart squeezed at the thought of Tank and those strong arms that used to hold her. It was her own fault that she was sitting here instead of by his side on the deck with their friends.

"Hey, what's wrong?" Jeff was looking over his menu, studying Maeve's face. Her green eyes were filled with pain.

"Nothing," she said lightly. "Just trying to decide if I should go for broke and get a big greasy bar burger or suffer with a salad."

"Bar burger," they both said together, then laughed.

"You have a great laugh, Maeve," Jeff said as he looked back down at his menu. It was an offhand comment, not sounding like a sleazy pick-up line. With that, Maeve decided to relax and just enjoy the evening with an acquaintance she thought she should get to know better.

An hour later, Maeve wiped her fingers on her napkin for the umpteenth time. True to the genre, Izzy's bar burgers were juicy and delicious. She enjoyed her time with Jeff. He was easygoing and interesting. He could hold a conversation and asked questions of her and shared about himself but didn't dominate the conversation like so many of the transplanted young businessmen who had come to this sleepy seaside village.

"You never told my why you came to Grey's Harbor," Maeve said, suddenly realizing she knew about his beer brewing hobby and his love of kayaking but didn't know what had brought him here.

"I had an internship my last year of college in a large architectural firm who had offices in Baltimore. I discovered I loved the ocean but wasn't fond of that big of a city. So, when I graduated from college, I started looking for a firm somewhere on the East Coast who did large projects but was headquartered in a small town. Not an easy find." He picked up his beer and drained the last of it. "The rest is history."

"Is living in a small quiet town like Grey's Harbor everything you hoped it would be?"

"It is. I grew up in a smallish town. I thought I wanted to live in a bigger city, enjoy the amenities that city living offered. Honestly, it grew old. I decided living within driving distance of a big city was good enough for me."

"Hi, Maeve." Tank's mellow voice still could make her stomach flip, but this time it hurt her heart, too.

"Hi, Tank." She smiled up at him, her eyes glistening slightly.

Jeff didn't miss the chemistry between them, but before it turned awkward, he stood and offered his hand to Tank.

"Hi. I'm Jeff Mitchell."

"Tank Harmond."

They shook hands sizing each other up. Jeff was no dummy. This was the guy Maeve dated, and by all indications, it was past tense.

"You're the architect who worked on the new health clinic out by the mall, aren't you?" Tank asked, surprising Jeff.

"Yeah, I'm lead on that project. Are you involved with it?" Jeff asked, gesturing for Tank to have a seat. Tank shook his head and declined.

"I work for Ryker Wynn. We're doing the interior finishes on that. I like what you did. You met all the requirements for a health facility but made it feel inviting and warm. So many of those places are cold."

"Thank you. That was my absolute intention." Jeff smiled at him. Tank's appearance was misleading. Obviously, this was a man who was intelligent and paid attention to details.

"Well, have good night," Tank said to Jeff, "Maeve..." his voice just dropped off as he made his way toward the men's room.

Izzy watch the exchange from the bar. What could have been an extremely awkward, volatile encounter had gone very well. She didn't like drama in her bar. She didn't expect it from her friends, but you never knew. She snagged the bill from the waitress and delivered it herself to Maeve's table.

"Can I get you anything else?" Izzy asked pleasantly, her eyes on Maeve. The girl was hurting, and the man sitting across the table from her wasn't oblivious to that fact.

"No, thank you, Izzy." As he handed her several bills Maeve protested.

"I've got my share," she said, reaching into her pocket.

"Not tonight," Jeff said firmly. "It's my treat. Tell you what, you can get the next one. Keep the change, Izzy." He was trying to put Maeve at ease and stop her from feeling awkward. Izzy was a pro at handling these situations.

"Thanks, Jeff." She patted Maeve on the shoulder. "It looks like it was good karma that you ran into a friend tonight. Everyone needs a friend now and then. Now I'm going to go chat Tank up. You have a good evening." She gave Maeve a quick hug and headed toward the bar. "Hey, Tank. You promised to move that big barrel for me out back. You slackin' on me?" She hooked her arm through his and led him back out to the deck chewing him out for breaking a promise.

3

*T*he morning breakfast crowd was thinning, and Maeve sat down at a booth near the window to go over the morning receipts. Susie brought her a steaming mug of coffee and a warm cinnamon roll.

"Oh no, Susie. Not the roll."

"Yes, the roll. Maeve, you've lost weight. You're not eating, and I'm worried about you. I know I might be overstepping my bounds, but you need to take care of yourself. Tank was, is a great guy, but Jeff isn't bad looking. But there is one thing I know, no man wants a bag of bones, now eat up." Susie put both hands on her hips and gave Maeve a defiant look, daring her to give her grief.

Maeve sighed and picked up the roll. A slow smile spread across her face with the first bite.

"Damn, that's good. God love Anna and her bakery! Thanks, Susie, and you're not overstepping your bounds. You're a friend, not just an employee. Thanks for watching out for me."

"It's nothing that you haven't done for me. Giving me the extra hours when Franklin got hurt saved us. We wouldn't have been able to pay our bills if it wasn't for you."

A new customer came in and Susie hurried over get their drink order. The bell over the door jingled again and Maeve looked up to see Ryker and Jennifer walk in. Ryker waved at her and steered Jennifer over.

"Oh my gosh, Anna's cinnamon rolls," Jenny exclaimed as she sat down at the booth, joining Maeve. "That's one thing I miss about working here is the smell of those rolls when they get delivered."

Maeve stacked her paperwork making room for Ryker and Jennifer. Ryker slid in next to Jennifer scooting her over.

"Can I get you one?" Susie asked coming over to see what they needed.

"Hey Susie, how's it going? How's Franklin?" Jennifer asked.

"He's healing. He's up and about and hopefully will be able to get back to work in a month or so. That'll be a blessing. The man is beginning to get on my nerves. He's bored and cranky and needs to feel like a man again taking care of his family."

"I can imagine how he feels," Ryker said, knowing he would go stir crazy if he was laid up. "Remember, if you guys need anything, please let me know. Promise?"

"I will, Ryker. Thanks. Now I know you well enough to know you're here looking for a late Saturday morning breakfast, right?"

"You got that right. Bacon, eggs over medium, hash browns, biscuit and a slice of ham."

"And hot sauce," Susie said, laughing. "Jennifer?"

Jennifer eyed the cinnamon roll, but she wanted a big breakfast, too.

"I'll just have what Ryker's having, minus the ham. Thanks, and coffee for the both of us."

"And a cinnamon roll," Ryker added, watching Jennifer's face. He knew it would happen. A slow smile spread on her face, lighting up the world. Ryker's heart swelled. For so long her face held shadows of hurt. The smiles were few and far between. Now they came easier and were genuine. Jennifer was grateful for any act of kindness shown her and that made him mad. She deserved so much more, and he was determined to make that happen.

"So, what brings you two in here? I know it's not just for breakfast. I can tell something's up."

"We're going to have a party," Jennifer said, her eyes dancing with excitement.

"I'm up for a party," Maeve said kindly, struck at how Jennifer looked like a child at Christmas. "What's the occasion?"

"I want to have an open house. I know the cabin has been finished for a while, but I hadn't finished decorating it, and just this morning, Ryker finished the outdoor patio and grill area."

"I think it's a wonderful idea. Is this my invitation?" Maeve asked.

"Yep. We're inviting all our friends. Can you make it next Saturday? I know it's short notice." The uncertainly of a social faux pas clouded Jennifer's face

"Of course. I'll be there," Maeve reassured her with a smile.

"Maeve..." Ryker started.

"Ryker, I know Tank will be invited. It's okay. We're both adults and know how to behave." She admonished her brother.

"I know, but it's only fair to let you know."

"How's he doing? Really?"

"You know Tank. He doesn't share his feelings. He's quiet. Maeve, you did what you needed to do for yourself. I think he understands that. Honestly, I think he loves you enough to let you go. It's just hard."

Maeve's eyes filled with tears. Jennifer reached across the table and took her hand.

"I'm sorry, Maeve. I don't know if this is the right time to say this or not. You know I'm not very good at stuff like this, but you are welcome to bring a date. Maybe that Jeff guy you've been seeing." She gave Maeve's hand a squeeze.

"Thanks, Jennifer. I'll think about it."

"And I'll give Tank a heads up. That way it won't be a surprise. Is that okay?"

"Yeah, it's probably a good idea. Thanks, Ryker."

Susie showed up with the plates of food, and Ryker dug into his eggs, spreading the yolk into his hash browns. Jennifer slid her eyes over to him, watching him attack his food. Instead of starting on hers, she reached out and tore a chunk off the cinnamon roll, popping it into her mouth.

"Life's too damn short not to eat dessert first," she said defensively, licking her fingers of the thick maple icing.

"You know what? You're right," said Ryker as he put down his fork and joined her.

"So, you're going to come, right?" Ryker asked Tank as they loaded the last sheet of drywall into the trailer getting it ready to move out to the job in the morning.

"Yeah. I'll come." Tank's face was a mask, but Ryker had known Tank since they were kids. He knew what was under the surface. "Maeve's going to be there, I'm sure."

It wasn't a question. He knew Ryker's sister would be at the party. That really wasn't what he was asking. Jaxx closed the door of the trailer watching the exchange with interest. He and Maddy had already accepted the invitation to the party, and Maddy had already voiced the question as to whether Maeve would bring the man she had been seen dining with around town.

"If you're asking if Maeve is going to bring a date, I would guess she is. Tank, she told you she was moving on. You knew it would happen."

"I know, and I hope she's happy," he growled. Ryker knew there was truth behind that statement. He knew that Tank loved Maeve and wanted what was best for her. He just didn't understand why Tank didn't realize he was the best thing for his sister.

Jaxx slapped Ryker on the back, a twisted grin on his face.

"My man, that boy is going to have to figure it out on his own. The question is, will it be too late?" He picked up his coffee thermos and gave a lazy wave to Ryker and Tank. "I'm out. Betty's going to need her beach walk, and I have date night with Maddy tonight. It's a rough job keeping up with three demanding females." He hopped in his truck and drove away, his hand hanging out the window in a farewell salute.

"I think the man's dog outweighs his girlfriend," Tank said thinking of the giant Bull Mastiff named Betty. "And their little girl has the man tied around her finger."

"The real question is who does he like more?" Ryker asked. "At least his wife can handle the competition." He had flashbacks of his jealous and controlling ex-girlfriend, Margot. She would not have waited for him while he gave his dog a long walk on the beach. Margot waited for no man. He considered himself very lucky to have gotten out of that situation before he made a mistake, and now he had Jenny. He hoped this party was all she had hoped for and more. If he had his way, it would be the best party ever. Jenny deserved it.

4

Saturday dawned sunny and warm. Jennifer woke to the smell of hickory smoke wafting through her window. She smiled. She had three pork shoulders packed in the smoker she had picked up on sale a couple of weeks ago. Despite a traumatic childhood at the hands of an abusive father, she had learned to smoke pork at an early age. Her daddy would go hunting for wild boar and smoking the meat low and slow made it tender and tasty. When Daddy bagged a boar, they didn't go hungry for a long time, and she could count on him being in a good mood for a least a couple of days.

While she didn't have wild boar, she did have three beautiful shoulders from a farm down the coast a ways. She was betting on it tasting as good as it smelled. She threw on a pair of sweats and her flip flops and she went outside to take a peek in the smoker. The meat was developing a good bark and the smell was heavenly. The meat had about four more hours to go, and then she would wrap it and let it sit before she shredded it into classic pulled pork. Her mouth watered thinking about it.

Going back into the cabin she consulted her timetable. She needed to get a shower and get to work if she wanted everything perfect for when her guests arrived. Suddenly her stomach turned cold. This wasn't her. Little Jennifer Creely didn't invite people to her house. She didn't let friends into her world. She didn't take that chance. This was a huge step for her. She wanted it, but out of the blue she was getting cold feet.

A shower would help. By the time she was done with that, Ryker would probably be here ready to help her set up, cook, or anything else she would need. Ryker would calm her down and fix everything. That easy, confident smile, those deep green eyes, and that strength that protected her would be here.

Hugging herself she stepped into the big open shower in the master bathroom. She had told Ryker that she wanted a shower so big that nothing would touch her when she was in there. Ryker gave her what she wanted. There was a wall she stepped around and then a big open space with high windows letting in light. She sighed as the hot water cascaded over her shoulders. She hadn't realized she was so tense. Maybe this party wasn't such a good idea. As much as she wanted to just stand there for an hour with the steam rising and the water washing away her fears, she knew she had a lot to do, so she cleaned up quickly and turned off the water. Stepping out, she wrapped herself in an oversized bath sheet, enjoying the secure cocoon it made around her.

She heard a knock at the door and stiffened, a lightning bolt of fear shooting through her body. She felt exposed and vulnerable.

"Jenny, honey, it's me," Ryker called out, knowing full well he needed to reassure her that it was only him at her home. Once, not so long ago, it had been someone else who was determined to hurt her very badly. He had managed to do a lot of damage, both physically and emotionally before he was stopped. Ryker had been working for months on end to make Jennifer feel comfortable and safe. She had come a long way, and he was proud of her, but there was always a spark of fear there, hiding under the surface, and it infuriated him.

"Where are you, sweetie?" he called again, not moving from the doorway.

"I just got out of the shower," she called.

Ryker moved further into the house now, knowing she knew who was there. He crossed through the great room and turned down the hall toward the master bedroom. Jennifer appeared at the doorway, a giant fluffy white towel encapsulating her body.

"Damn, Jenny, we've got work to do and you greet me like that?" he teased her as he wrapped her in his arms, pulling her toward him. She smelled of coconut and lime, and her skin was silky and soft. He hated the fact that she stiffened for a brief second as he pulled her close, but a second later she melted into him. *Baby steps,* he thought.

He combed his fingers through her damp hair, working out the tangles as she snuggled into his chest. He wanted nothing more than to pick her up and carry her into the bedroom, laying her out on that big four poster bed she bought at the antique shop a month ago. He wanted to lay her back and cover every part of that sweet smelling body with kisses.

"Hey, now," she said smiling up shyly at him. "I don't think we have time to do what you're thinking."

"How do you know what I'm thinking?" He growled into her hair, moaning at the images his mind was offering him.

"It's pretty obvious," she said laughing.

"Is it now?"

"It is."

He bent his lips to hers.

And with that their schedule went all to hell.

*J*ennifer looked around for the umpteenth time. Her nerves were stringing tighter and tighter. The guests were set to arrive in a half an hour, and she was sure she was forgetting something.

"It's going to be okay, you know that, right?" Ryker asked as he added more ice to the tub holding bottles of beer.

"I guess," she said, pacing the patio, centering the flowers on the table, moving a chair over an inch.

"What worries you the most?" he asked, pulling her into him and stroking her hair. "It's just a party."

"I've never had a party before."

Damn it. He'd missed it. It never dawned on him. *Of course, growing up the way she did, she was lucky to eat and have clothes much less have a party.*

"Well, I promise you, this won't be your last party, but it's going to be one of the best." He tilted her chin up so he could look her in the eyes. "Jenny, I promise I won't let you down. Your home looks perfect, the food is going to be great, and you're beautiful." He kissed her deeply willing confidence into her soul.

Suddenly she pulled away and squealed.

"Honey, what's wrong? What happened?" Ryker frantically looked her over to see what hurt her.

"I forgot to set the timer for the potatoes." She turned from him and ran into the house, certain her cheesy potatoes would be burned.

Ryker followed her at a much slower pace, knowing full well that there was no catastrophe in the making. Poor Jennifer was beside herself, but by the end of this day, he was sure, at least he hoped he was sure, she would be a much more secure lady.

A vehicle pulled into the driveway, the first of their guests arriving. Jennifer came out on the deck in time to see Tank stepping out of his truck. In one hand he held a beautifully wrapped basket.

"Hello, beautiful," he said as he walked up the stone path to the patio. He kissed Jennifer on the cheek and handed her the basket.

"Tank, you didn't need to bring anything," she blushed, unsure of what to do.

"I didn't need to, darlin', I wanted to," he said sincerely, holding her eyes with his. He shared Ryker's anger, remembered seeing her bruised body when they were in high school. She had been swimming in the river, not knowing anyone was around, When she took off her clothes and stood in the sun with only a bathing suit on, the ugly evidence of the kind of life she endured was painted in vivid blues and purples all over her. If the man who did it to her wasn't dead, Tank would have gladly helped Ryker make the guy disappear. Tank smiled at her, knowing he had upset her balance, but wanting to put her at ease.

"Well, thank you," she said as she gleefully opened the cellophane wrapping. "These smell amazing," she exclaimed as she held up a silky bar of handmade soap. "I want to go take a bath right now and use one of them!" She was delighted with the gift, and Tank knew that he had to remember to thank his friend Maddy for the guidance. He would have blundered it all on his own.

"Have a beer, Tank," said Ryker, slapping his best friend on the back. Jennifer scooted into the house taking the basket of soaps into her master bath. She checked her reflection in the mirror and was surprised at the person looking back at her. She almost didn't recognize herself. She looked happy. She decided she liked that look.

She checked on the food in the kitchen, backing the oven temperature to warm. Then she pulled a large tray of cured meats and cheeses out of the fridge. Balancing the tray on one hand and snagging a basket of assorted crackers with the other, she made her way back out to the patio.

Jaxx Stockman opened the door for her and took the tray out of her hands. Jennifer was surprised to see how many people were already there. Maddy Grey gave her a kiss and took the crackers from her, too, then handed her a chilled bottle of white wine. Within minutes Jennifer was surrounded with friends and well-wishers all bearing small, thoughtful gifts, many asking to see the cabin now that it was finished.

She and Ryker gave tours while her guests oohed and ahed over the homey touches Jennifer had layered over Ryker's fine craftsmanship. The cabin wasn't large, but it was gracious and warm; a perfect place on the river for Jennifer.

"Hey, sweetie, do you need any help with the food?" Jennifer turned around from showing a guest the mantle Ryker had carved to see Maeve smiling at her with Jeff by her side.

"No, thank you. Well, maybe." Jennifer suddenly felt insecure realizing it was time to bring out the food.

"Come on, honey, you've got this," Maeve said kindly. She took

Jennifer's hand and led her to the kitchen. "What are we having today?"

When Maeve caught sight of the amount of food Jennifer had put together, she enlisted the help of Jeff, Ryker, and Bridger, who were standing in the living room telling lies to each other. She tossed each of them a set of potholders and pointed to the steaming dishes of food.

"Take those outside boys, and don't drop them," she ordered them with mock authority.

"Please put them on the long bar out there," Jennifer suggested. When they designed the patio, Jennifer told Ryker she had always wanted to be able to have friends come and eat outside with her. She wanted a huge long table where everyone could sit, and she wanted a place where she could grill and serve food. Of course, Ryker had come through for her. Eventually, there would be a pavilion roof over the table to protect it and the guests from the elements, but for now, the sun was shining, and the trees provided adequate shade. Jennifer followed the line of men. She was carrying two baskets of homemade breads and could hardly see because of the tears welling up in her eyes. She couldn't believe everyone came to her party. She was over-whelmed. Someone took the baskets from her hands and she turned and fled back into the kitchen. She tried to get herself under control so no one would see her.

"Jennifer? Honey, are you okay?"

She didn't turn around. She wasn't sure who was asking her, but she didn't want them to see her with tears in her eyes. She nodded and tried to busy herself, wiping the counter with the dishcloth.

"I'm fine, thank you," she said, her voice not as steady as she had hoped.

"Jennifer, all the people here are your friends. We all love you and want to celebrate your new home. But we also want you to know we will always be here for you. Anytime you need any of us, you just need to call. I'm just across the river. I'll always come running."

Bridger.

She turned and gave him a weak smile, tears brimming in her eyes.

"Thank you, Bridger. I'm just a little overwhelmed."

"I know, honey. Remember when we all came to help you at the old cabin? Remember when you threw a tablecloth on that ancient table and we grilled burgers on that old grill? This is no different. It's still just a bunch of friends eating together. Then, we celebrated working together. Today, we celebrate being together. You've got this, kiddo. And honestly, what you don't have, we have for you. You good?" Bridger asked kindly.

Jennifer swiped at her eyes, smiled and nodded.

"I'm good."

"Hey, Bridger, are you moving in on my lady? You've got Hope. Back off my girl," Ryker teased him. Ryker sized up the situation and knew that whatever had happened, Bridger had it under control. Ryker slipped his arm around Jennifer's waist.

"Are you ready, sweetie? Let's party before this food gets cold." He kissed her on the forehead and led her out the door onto the patio and into the warmth of a circle of friends.

5

"*H*ey, Jennifer, you wanted to try out your new fire pit, right?" Tank called to Jennifer as he snagged another beer from the tub.

Jennifer and Ryker were hand in hand walking toward the riverbank. She stopped and turned, her face lined with worry.

"I did, but I forgot to get wood," Jennifer replied, suddenly realizing that was on her list but she had somehow missed it.

"No worries, the back of my truck is loaded with wood. Is it okay if we set up a fire?"

"It's more than okay. It's perfect." She started to walk toward them to help, but Ryker pulled at her hand, setting her back on the path toward the river.

"Tank, can I help you with that?" Jeff asked. Maeve watched warily from the porch rocker she was sitting in.

"Sure, I would welcome the help."

The two men moved off toward the truck together. Jaxx looked over at Maeve and nudged Maddy.

"I don't think they're going to kill each other," Jaxx said. "They wouldn't ruin Jennifer's party."

"I know. It just feels so awkward."

"Tank is trying, Maeve," Maddy offered. "He has been a perfect gentleman today. I don't think you have to worry."

"I know. Tank is…well Tank is Tank. Jeff is just from a different world. He doesn't speak Tank's language," she said, not really sure what she was worried about.

"Maeve, they're both grown men. Tank'll be fine. We all respect your decisions and will stand by you, and so will Tank. You have to know that about him. He only wants you to be happy, and if Jeff makes you happy, Tank will respect that," Bridger said, watching his friend carry wood to the pit.

"But we all know Tank is hurting, too, Maeve. In fact, you're both miserable," said Hope pointing out the obvious that no one else wanted to mention.

"Oh, what a mess," Maeve said. "I'm going to have another glass of wine. Anyone care to join me?" She held up the bottle as an invitation. Both Maddy and Hope leaned forward offering their glasses for another fill-up.

Bridger and Jaxx decided that Tank and Jeff needed guidance in fire starting, so they left the girls to gossip and wandered over to the pit.

*s the party everything you had hoped?" Ryker asked Jennifer as they watched the river flow slowly by on its way to the ocean.

"It is," she said, her eyes shining with delight. "At least it was once I started to relax. I don't know what came over me," she admitted.

"I'm glad you were nervous. It means you care. You were nervous because you wanted it to be perfect for your guests. It's because you care about each and every one of them. That's what I love about you, Jenny. You care. Let's be honest. No one would fault you if you became the kind of person who didn't care about others. You have been hurt by so many people that you have every right to hate people and not ever give of yourself. But you're not like that. You care deeply. And you love deeply. I love that so much about you."

He turned her to face him. The sun was low in the sky, lighting the world in a soft glow. It turned Jennifer's skin a soft rosy pink. A light breeze picked up a strand of hair, moving it across her face. Ryker reached up and smoothed it away. He brushed her lips with his thumb, then bent his mouth to hers and kissed her softly.

"You know I love you, don't you Jenny?"

She nodded, her eyes large and luminous.

"I love you more than life itself. I never really knew the meaning of love until I saw you again, when you came back to Grey's Harbor. I knew then I wanted to protect you and take care of you. But what I didn't know is that I needed your love more than you needed mine. Jenny, you saved me. You taught me what love really is, and I can't imagine my life without you."

Jennifer stared at him, her eyes brimming with tears,

"Jenny," Ryker dropped to one knee and took her left hand. "I asked you before, but you weren't ready. You asked for time. I've given that to you, but I don't want to wait any longer. Would you please marry me and make me the happiest man on earth?" He slipped a ring on her finger, his eyes never leaving hers.

She sank to the ground in front of him. She put her hands on each side of his face and looked him in the eyes.

He waited. His heart beating out of his chest.

"I love you, Ryker Wynn. And yes, I will marry you."

And then she kissed him, and Ryker knew that all he had done before this moment was erased. From here on, they were together forever.

"*M*aeve..." Hope touched Maeve's arm bringing her attention away from Tank and Jeff's attempt at making the fire.

"Hmmm?" she asked.

"Look toward the river. Look at your brother."

Maddy followed Hope's gaze and saw it the same time Maeve did.

"Am I seeing what I think I'm seeing?" Maeve asked.

They watched as Jennifer sank to the ground in front of Ryker, both now on their knees.

"My guess is yes, and my guess is she said yes," said Maddy, a sentimental tear running down her cheek.

"Honey, why are you crying?" Jaxx asked just joining the girls having started the fire with one match.

"Look," she said, gesturing to the river.

"So, Ryker and Jennifer are kissing. That's nothing new. I don't know why they have to do it on their knees in the grass but whatever trips their trigger," he said, helping himself to a brownie.

"Dense male," Maeve snorted.

"Who's a dense male?" asked Bridger, joining Jaxx on the patio and grabbing a brownie, too.

"Most of them," Hope replied.

Bridger shook his head, then realized they were all looking at the river. He took in the scene and looked at the girls' faces.

"Hmmm… my guess is Ryker finally asked that girl to marry him," Bridger said simply, biting into the brownie. "Wow, these are good. Are they Anna's?"

"No, I think Jennifer made them."

"Damn, Ryker's a lucky man," he said appreciating the brownie even more.

Tank and Jeff joined the group.

"Jaxx got the fire started if you want to move the chairs over to the bonfire," Tank suggested.

"Sounds like a plan," Maeve said, suddenly ready to draw the attention away from the happy couple. She was well aware that an announcement would soon follow, and she wasn't sure how she was going to handle it. She was ecstatic for her brother and friend, but the wound in her heart cut even deeper.

Maddy grabbed her chair, too, following Maeve. She was acutely aware of the pain Maeve was feeling. She also knew that there was nothing anyone would be able to say to help.

6

*T*he party was winding down, and Maeve was helping Jennifer in the kitchen. Jennifer was tired but incredibly happy.

"I am thrilled for you and Ryker. You guys are perfect together," Maeve said, kindly.

"Thank you, Maeve. I keep pinching myself. I can't believe this is actually happening to me." She looked down and stared at the glittery diamond on her finger. Maeve looked at it, too, with a pang in her heart. Despite her pain, Maeve smiled. She was glad her brother found Jennifer and wasn't with Margot anymore. Although the ring on Jennifer's finger was beautiful, it would never have been up to Margot's standards. Jennifer was more grounded, and she appreciated everything Ryker did for her.

"Well, honey, it's real. Ryker doesn't do anything he isn't totally committed to, and once he makes a decision, he moves forward fast."

"No kidding. He doesn't want to wait to get married."

"Wait, when are you guys thinking of doing this?"

"He said tomorrow, but I told him I needed a little more time." Jennifer grinned, conspiratorially. "I mean, I have to shop for a dress, right?"

"Absolutely, and venues are always booked way in advance."

"Oh, no, Maeve, we don't want a big wedding. I want to get married on the beach. I mean, we haven't had time to talk about any of this, but I'm pretty sure Ryker would go for that."

"Honey, Ryker would go for anything that would make you happy. Don't you know that yet?" Maeve wiped her hands on a dish cloth and took Jennifer's hands in hers. "My brother loves you very much. It has been obvious to all of us for some time. He deserves happiness and you've given that to him. He would go to the ends of the earth to make sure he's given you everything you could ever want. All I ask is that you make my brother happy. He means the world to me."

"I promise you, Maeve. I will." Jennifer looked at the ring again. "Maeve, would you please help me find a dress? Would you mind?"

"Of course, I would love to, but wouldn't you rather have…" then she stopped herself, remembering that Jennifer had no one. "I would be honored."

"Can I ask you something else?" Jennifer said, her head bowed slightly, unsure of herself.

Maeve's heart broke. *Would this girl ever be totally confident and secure?* Maybe never, but she was determined to help bring her as far as humanly possible.

"You can ask me anything. Always."

"Would you please be my Maid of Honor?" Jennifer smiled at her shyly.

"Oh honey, it would be my pleasure. I'd love to." Maeve wrapped her arms around Jennifer and hugged her tightly. "I just realized I'm going to get a sister!"

I can't believe you're going to beat me to the altar," Bridger said, remembering his proposal to Hope in the hospital.

"Long engagements are for the birds," Ryker teased Bridger enjoying the fact that he had one-upped his buddy.

"Hope wanted a spring wedding, so you know, the bride kinda

calls the shots."

"No kidding. I told Jenny I wanted to get married tomorrow, but she put her foot down." They all smiled at that image. Jeff walked over to Tank's truck to get another armload of wood.

"Good girl," said Tank. "She's going to have to learn to put her foot down a lot with you as her husband. "She's come a long way, Ryker. You've been good for that girl. I can't believe she's the same person we knew in high school."

"She's not," said Ryker seriously.

"I didn't know her in high school," Jaxx said, "but I can tell she's a vulnerable person, yet, I can also tell that there is a hell of a lot of strength in there."

"You don't know the half of it," Bridger said. "Tank, you'll be my best man, and Bridger and Jaxx, you'll stand with me, right?

"Of course," they all agreed and raised a glass to celebrate.

Hope and Maddy looked at each other. They were sitting in chairs in the perimeter of the fire ring, temporarily forgotten by the men.

"This should be interesting," said Maddy to Hope.

"What?" Hope asked, watching Bridger with a smile on her face thinking about her upcoming spring wedding.

"Well, I'm pretty sure we can count on Jennifer to ask Maeve to be her Maid of Honor, don't you think?"

"Of course," Hope said, as if there were no other choice. "Oh, shit."

"Exactly, Tank is the best man. That'll be extremely interesting."

"What'll be interesting? Jeff asked as he returned with a few logs.

"Oh, just wedding preparations," Hope said sweetly. "You know, male versus female ideas and all that."

"No, I don't know, and I'm not sure I want to," Jeff teased and moved over to the fire to add the armload of logs.

*A*s the last of the guests pulled away, Ryker reached for Jennifer's hand and walked her up to the patio. The embers in the fire were a memory, doused thoroughly with water, and the last of the empty beer bottles had been gathered.

"Happy?" he asked her, marveling at how beautiful she looked in the moonlight.

"Very, thank you," she said as she lay her head on his shoulder and looked out over the river. She had a beautiful cabin with a wonderful place to gather with friends, and now she had a future with the man she loved and trusted with all her heart.

"Are you excited about the wedding? I saw you with the girls, your heads all together. It was obvious you were planning and plotting."

"They wanted to know when we planned on getting married. I was worried when I told them soon."

"Why were you worried, honey?"

"Because Bridger proposed to Hope, but they're not getting married until the spring. I didn't want to do anything that would hurt her feelings."

"And what did she say when you told her we wanted to get married soon?"

Jennifer smiled with the memory.

"She asked me how she could help. I asked her if she was upset and she just laughed and said that she would learn from my mistakes."

"That's good, right?" Ryker asked, unsure of the workings of women.

"Yes, that was good." Jennifer reassured him. "Seriously though, when you said tomorrow, I know you were kidding, but when are you thinking?"

"As soon as you can pull it together. Honey, I just want a life with you. I know that you don't have any family, and most everyone I want to invite is here in Grey's Harbor. I know you'd like to get married on the beach, and I think it's great. What do you think about having the reception at Cadigan's Marina? Bridger said he could clear an area. There would be plenty of room for dancing." He looked at her, nervous that his plain ideas wouldn't be right for his bride. Thoughts of socialite Margot swam in his head and he groaned thinking he might have just made a mistake voicing the marina idea.

"Ryker, that would be wonderful. I think having the reception at the marina could be fun. I was afraid you would want something fancy at the country club or something. I don't want to spend that kind of money, and I would feel so awkward. Ryker, I just want to be surrounded by my friends, and I just want to have another party to celebrate like we had today. Only this time, I don't want to cook." She grinned up at Ryker suddenly realizing that she pulled off her first party and it was a success.

"Deal. You don't have to cook. Okay, married on the beach, soon, reception at the marina. What else do we have to do?"

"Truthfully Bridger, I don't know. Unlike most girls who dreamed of their wedding since they were a child, I just dreamt of being somewhere other than Grey's Harbor."

Ryker's heart squeezed thinking of the abused little girl who didn't have romantic visions of one day marrying her prince, but rather squeezed her eyes shut and dreamt of a time when a man wouldn't be abusing her. *Damn it,* he wished he could erase the past.

"Ryker," Jennifer said, smoothing his creased forehead with her fingertips, "it's okay. I found my way back home to you. I love Grey's Harbor now, and I love you. I trust you, and I know that my life is going to be amazing." She raised her lips to his and kissed him gently. "Besides, I asked your sister to be my Maid of Honor. She's capable of anything, so I'm fairly certain she can tap into her childhood wedding dreams and help me plan ours."

"My sister?" Ryker echoed, his mind turning with the ramifications. *Well, this could be fun,* he thought. "Yeah, my sister is full of wedding ideas you can tap. She'll be great."

Jennifer nodded, then suddenly yawned.

"Oh, excuse me," she said, surprised.

Ryker suddenly realized how tired she was. Despite the fact that he wanted a repeat performance of this morning, he was determined to tuck his lady into bed so she could drift off to some sweet dreams for once.

7

"*I*s it going to awkward for you?' Jeff asked as he twirled Maeve's hair with his fingers. She sighed against his chest.

"I don't know. I hope not. I don't want anything to ruin that day for Jennifer."

"Honestly, Maeve, Tank seems like a pretty decent guy. I know he was hurt when you left him, but he's a gentleman. I'm pretty certain it'll be fine." Jeff looked down at the woman he was holding in his arms. It was a warm night, and they were leaning against the foundations of the old lighthouse. It was dark, no moon lit the sky. The waves lapped softly just inches from their feet, the tide high but the ocean calm

"He will be," Maeve agreed. *It's just that I might not.* Her heart squeezed in her chest at the thought of standing up with Tank, but not for the reason she had always dreamed. It was now just a memory and she had to move on. She turned and smiled up at Jeff.

His chin and throat, shaved that morning, were there, inviting her to kiss them, so she turned her attention to the man who was with her, the man who was turning out to be a wonderful date and devoted... *partner*? No, she was not yet ready to call him a partner, but he was a close friend and getting closer.

She felt Jeff shift, the intensity of his kisses amplified, his hands roving, surer of himself than the other times they had begun to explore intimacy. She responded, then felt herself pull back, not ready to go any further. Jeff, intent on investigating her mouth and her breasts, wasn't aware of the shift in her. She pulled back gently, still giving him a kiss as an apology.

"I'm sorry, Jeff. I'm just not… ready…" she left the rest unsaid.

He took a half a second to bring himself under control. After all, that's what he did best. He knew in order to succeed in business, you had to read your players and not rush the deal. He didn't want to blow it with Maeve. She was a remarkable woman, kind and beautiful. An asset to his future. He very much wanted her in his future, so he took a deep breath and calmed himself, then turned a smiling face toward her.

She could tell he was smiling in the dark, his straight white teeth gleaming despite the lack of a moon to light the night.

"Bridger wanted to know if we wanted to go sailing with them on Saturday. Ryker and Jennifer are going, and, of course, Hope."

"Um...sure," said Jeff, unwilling to let Maeve know that being on a boat in the ocean was not his idea of fun. Just the thought of being out of control and at the mercy of the waves made him break out in a cold sweat, but he knew when he moved to the coast that these opportunities would present themselves. One day it might be a client offering, and he needed to be smooth and comfortable should the occasion arise. Plus, Maeve's eyes were sparkling at the idea.

"Are you sure? You seem hesitant," she asked, not wanting to push him.

"No, I just had to run through my calendar in my head and make sure I didn't have any conflicts. I think we're good to go. Just tell me what time to pick you up and what I need to bring, and I'll be there ready to float your boat." He grinned, feeling witty but just not brave.

"I'll tell Bridger it's a go and give you the details later. Ready to walk back? I have an early morning tomorrow. The breakfast crowd waits for no woman."

"Maeve," Jeff asked suddenly, "do you really like working that hard all the time? The diner has to monopolize your time like no other job." He thought about her at home, waiting for him to arrive, dressed and ready to go out on the town. To see and be seen. He loved the night life and moving through a crowd, and he wanted Maeve on his arm to share that with him.

"It's a lot of work, but it's a labor of love. Ever since I can remember I wanted to own a restaurant. I tried every recipe I could get my hands on when I was a kid, keeping the winners in a little recipe card box." She smiled wistfully at the memory.

"Did any of those childhood recipes make the cut?" Jeff asked amused and touched by her child-like enthusiasm.

"My warm gingerbread with lemon sauce was one of those such recipes. When I make it, I sell out so fast that if I don't grab a slice before I make it available, I won't even get any, and it's one of my favorites."

"That sounds delicious. You're going to have to tell me when it's going to be on the menu again so I can try it."

"And how do you feel about biscuits and sausage gravy?" she asked seriously.

"Truthfully, I've never had it. The concoction always looks so…"

"Like chewed up dog food?" Maeve supplied.

"Kinda…not really appealing."

"Stop around for breakfast tomorrow morning. You're in for a treat," she said solemnly, like he was about to partake in a religious experience.

"I don't know," he started.

"Nonsense. I'm open early enough for you to eat a leisurely break-fast and get to your office with plenty of time."

Like the boat, this was something Jeff knew he was going to have to do if he had any hope at all to seal any future deals.

"Somehow, I think I'm going to be needing more time scheduled at the gym if we keep hanging out together," Jeff said, patting his trim waist without an ounce of fat.

Like Tank, he was fit, but there was a difference. Tank was solid,

Jeff was just trim. Neither carried extra fat, but Tank was just more…there.

Maeve unwound herself from Jeff and stood up, stretching. She brushed the sand off her butt and picked up the sandals she had previously shed. Jeff stood up next to her.

"Ready to go? We can walk to my car and I can drive you home," Jeff said taking her hand in his. She noticed that his hands weren't much bigger than hers, and soft, his nails well-kept. She remembered how tiny her hands felt in Tank's, his rough calloused skin telling tales of hard work. *Damn, he was on her mind tonight. It wasn't fair to Jeff.*

"You don't have to drive me home, I can walk. Besides, you have to get up early so you can get your biscuits and gravy in the morning." She smiled wickedly at him.

"Absolutely not. You aren't walking home alone in the dark. Maeve, that's not safe," Jeff said squeezing her hand.

"I've walked alone in the dark all my life, Jeff. This is Grey's Harbor."

"Still, not on my watch, Maeve. I want to take care of you and protect you, even if you don't need protecting. Let me do that for you, please?" He turned her to face him. "Please," he said again.

"Okay," she agreed, allowing him to kiss her again to seal the deal. He took her hand in his again and led her to his car, feeling like they were getting closer, like he might have a chance with this remarkable woman after all.

He opened the passenger door for her, helping her in, and she watched him walk around the front of the car, lit by the streetlight. He was so sweet, so attentive. Why didn't her heart sing with happiness? Any woman would feel lucky to have a man like Jeff; successful, good looking, kind, gentle, attentive. Why did her heart keep resisting and her head keep bringing Tank to the front of her mind? Tank didn't want a commitment, couldn't love her enough for that. She had to move past it. She had to move on. She had to.

He opened the door and slipped in beside her, sliding the key into the ignition. The dome light lit her face. There was an odd, determined smile there.

"What?" Jeff questioned, unwilling to back out of the parking place with her looking at him like that.

"It would probably be easier for you to have breakfast at the diner if you had someone to help you wake up on time in the morning," Maeve suggested, her right eyebrow cocked upward.

His heart quickened. Could she actually be asking him to stay the night?

"Maeve, what are you saying?" he asked cautiously, afraid to hope.

"I'm saying would you like to spend the night?"

"I thought you weren't ready. You told me that."

"I'm a woman. I can change my mind. Now all we need to decide is your place or mine." She smiled at him, convincing herself that this is what she needed to move on.

8

"Good morning, beautiful lady," Jeff said, smiling down at Maeve as her alarm sounded on her phone.

"I didn't expect that," Maeve said, stretching her back, unaccustomed to a softer bed than her own.

"Didn't expect what?" Jeff said, nuzzling her neck, "Although I'd like to think there were a lot of things you didn't expect last night," he said. Maeve thought he sounded almost too hopeful. *Insecure,* she wondered.

"I didn't expect you to be more cheerful than me in the morning. I don't know, I didn't peg you for a morning guy."

"Au contraire, I am an anytime guy." He wagged his eyebrows at her in a Groucho Marx kind of way. "Do you have time, beautiful?" he asked playfully, reaching for her breasts.

"Unfortunately, no," she said firmly, not feeling the same disappointment that showed in his eyes. "I have breakfasts to cook and lunch food to prep. I need to be out of here in fifteen minutes. Can you do that, or should I call for a ride?" she asked as she headed toward his bathroom and turned on the shower.

"I'll drive you, but the diner doesn't open for another hour, right?" he asked, looking at the clock.

"True, but I have a lot to get done before I open the doors. You are welcome to sit in a booth and wait," she said, the ramifications of that dawning on her as the words came out of her mouth.

"Yeah, how about I drop you, buy a newspaper and then show up when you are officially open?"

"Sounds like a better plan." She tested the water and stepped in the shower. She felt guilty that her mind was grateful that the shower felt so necessary after last night. She was a willing participant. She wasn't forced, yet she suddenly felt the urge to scrub away the experience.

She closed her eyes and let the water pour over the top of her head cascading down her face and across her breasts, which were suddenly being soaped up by two hands, the rest of the body followed pressing against her suggestively. She opened her eyes to see Jeff in all his morning glory grinning at her holding a loofah.

Inwardly, she groaned. Yet, she wanted this relationship, right? Intimacy was a part of a loving relationship. She had to move on. Just move on.

"It'll have to be quick," she said, "and I mean quick."

*D*amn it," Maeve swore as she took the overly brown biscuits out of the oven. "Unbelievable," she muttered.

"What is with you this morning?" Susie asked, quickly grabbing the next tray of biscuits and sliding them into the oven. "I don't think I've ever seen you burn biscuits before. What gives? And give that gravy a stir," she said pointing to the pot on the stove.

Maeve moved over and picked up the large stainless-steel spoon, stirring the silky gravy and making certain it wasn't sticking to the bottom of the pot. The gravy had thickened perfectly, and Maeve tested it to see if she had enough pepper in it. She did. She turned the burner to the lowest setting and turned to face Susie.

"I'm sorry, I'm just distracted."

"I think you're missing Tank. I know it's none of my business, but there, I said it. Jeff's a great guy, but you and Tank, there's something special there," Susie said as she measured out flour for Maeve to make up another batch of biscuits.

"Tank and I are through, Susie. You can romanticize all you want, but we're no longer an item. End of discussion. Understand?" Maeve held Susie's eyes with hers until Susie squirmed a little.

"Sorry. I didn't mean to overstep."

"No, I'm sorry. I know you're just being a friend. I get it, but really, I've moved on, Susie. It's for the best, and Jeff really is a great guy. In fact, he's coming in to try the biscuits 'n gravy. Apparently, he's never had it before. Said it looks like chewed up dog food, so he wouldn't consider eating it."

"I always thought it looked kinda like cat barf, but to each his own," Susie said grinning. "Best tasting cat barf this side of the Mississippi, though."

"I think that was a compliment," Maeve said slowly.

"Yep, it was, and there's your new man now. Shall I seat him, or are you all over that?" Susie said, the double meaning completely clear.

"I may have been all over that once or twice," Maeve threw over her shoulder. *There, that should get the tongues wagging,* she thought. *It'll help me move on. Just move on,* her mantra playing in her head as she put a smile on her face and made her way across the restaurant to meet Jeff.

"Bar, table, or booth?" she asked.

"Bar, unless you planned on joining me."

"Bar then, because I have too much to do to stop and have some breakfast, but this way I'll be able to see your face when you try my breakfast special."

"Okay, bring it on."

"An order of biscuits and gravy coming up. Orange juice or coffee?"

"Small orange juice, coffee with cream and sugar," he said, glancing at the bar first to see if creamers were already there. *Tank likes it black,* she thought. *Where did that come from and why does it matter?* she chided herself. *Drinking coffee black does not make you manly.*

"Got it. I'll be right back." As she went into the kitchen the diner door opened again, bringing six more customers in. She looked over at Susie and Pete, her cook who had just come in. "Okay folks, it's showtime."

"*W*ell?" asked Maeve as Jeff set his fork down and wiped his mouth with a napkin. "What'd you think?"

"That was amazing. I can't believe I've never tried this stuff. It's fantastic."

"Old-fashioned, depression comfort food," she said with a smile on her face. "Maybe your family didn't eat that way."

"Mom never made this, but it reminds me a little of my mom's chipped beef over toast." He smiled at the memory; one he had forgotten. His palate was much more sophisticated than his childhood tastes.

"I love chipped beef over toast with the white sauce," Maeve said, her mind already working on offering it as a breakfast special next week.

"Yep that's the stuff. It was pretty good." Jeff stood up. "I need my check so I can get going." He patted his pockets going through a check in his mind, *keys, phone, wallet.*

"It's on me this morning." Maeve smiled warmly at him, then laughed as his brow creased and he started to protest. "Don't worry. It won't happen again. My generosity doesn't overshadow my good business sense."

"Okay, then thank you," he said graciously, then looked at her trying to figure out just how to kiss her goodbye. She read his mind and shook her head slightly, glancing around the diner. There were several pairs of interested eyes unabashedly watching them.

"You're welcome, and I'll catch you later. Have a good day," Maeve called over her shoulder as she turned to get the coffee pot so she could fill her curious customers empty mugs.

9

"Okay, I'm here. What did you need from me?" Jaxx asked Maddy as he walked up behind her and reached his arms around her, pulling her back against him. Betty, his huge mastiff bound past them and started nipping at the waves. Jaxx nibbled her neck, squeezing her gently. "Didn't get enough of me this morning, eh?"

"I can never get enough of you, but that's not why I asked you out here. You got here earlier than I expected. You usually work with Ryker until later." She turned around and snuggled against his shoulder, enjoying the closeness.

They were standing on the dunes overlooking the ocean. Jaxx had found her there after checking her studio and finding it empty. Gulls wheeled overhead and waves crashed against the sand, the tide rushing in restlessly. Betty ran back and forth chasing seagulls and receding waves. Belle sat in the sand waving her chubby fists, a plastic shovel grasped in one hand, a handful of sand grasped in the other. He kissed his baby on the top of her head then stood up and turned to Maddy.

"What's on your mind, baby?" Jaxx asked looking down into Maddy's dark eyes.

"Do you know how to weld?" she asked abruptly.

"Uh-oh, you have a creative idea in that pretty head of yours and it's going to involve me, isn't it?"

"Pretty much," she said agreeably, then turned again, leaning back against him so they could both look out over the water and keep an eye on Belle.

"Okay, yes I can weld. I don't have any equipment, but I'm sure Ryker has what I need. If he doesn't, I'm pretty positive I can locate some."

"That won't be necessary. I bought a welder this morning," she said simply, still not looking at him.

"You bought a welder, but you don't know how to weld?"

"Pretty much," she said again. "But I'm willing to learn."

Jaxx turned her around to face him grinning at the smile he saw playing on her lips.

"Time to spill it, Maddy. What are you cooking up?" He knew she had some big plans. He could feel it, and he loved it. He knew the kind of art she was capable of producing, and he really enjoyed watching her create.

"Come on up to the studio and take a look at my sketches." She picked up Belle, who set up a wail of protest, causing Betty to come galloping back to see who was assaulting her girl. Jaxx took Belle from Maddy's arms and lifted her to the sky, blowing a raspberry against her belly. Belle squealed in a wave of giggles. Maddy grabbed Jaxx's hand and led him up the dune path to the little studio next to her cottage.

Inside, she rolled out the large sketch and put it down on the partner's desk she used as a cutting table. Jaxx gave a low whistle.

"That looks like a huge undertaking." He studied the drawings. The sketch showed a large, metal arched, three-dimensional frame supporting a huge set of arched panels of fused glass. The glass was an intricate design of the ocean with seagulls and starfish, sand dollars and dolphins.

Maddy waited quietly while Jaxx carefully looked over what she had. He handed Belle to her and picked up a pencil. He raised his eyebrow at her. She nodded. He quickly added a few lines here and there.

"You need more diagonal supports just to make sure it can handle the weight. Obviously, you can make them more decorative."

"I see what you're talking about. I would love to forge the pieces so they are graceful and attractive, but I'm not that good at working the metal yet." She sighed, her frustration at her limitations showing.

"Did you ask Donovan to help you?" Jaxx asked thinking of the young blacksmith artist who was staying at the artist retreat that Maddy owned.

"No, I didn't want to impose." She smiled wickedly.

"But you'll impose on me for the welding," Jaxx teased.

"I'm not sleeping with him." She bit her lip and stared at him, waiting to see how he would take the teasing.

"Hmmm. I knew I would have to pay up at some point," he teased back. "Let me guess, you accepted a commission for a garden gate, figuring you would manage to pull it off somehow." He remembered how she had agreed to repair the old stained glass windows in Mirabelle Grey's Victorian painted lady with no idea how she was going to transport them to her studio or where she was going to get a work table big enough to repair them all. But Maddy was resourceful, and she pulled it off without a hitch and with the help of some of her closest friends.

"Nope. This is even better. It's my...our...wedding gift to Jennifer and Ryker. I want to plant it on the beach where they're going to get married."

"They can get married under it," Jaxx said, the image forming in his head.

"Only if they want to. Or it can serve as an entrance arch. What-ever they want. Later it can go in their garden or in their trash." Maddy said. "I don't believe in imposing on anyone else's sense of decor."

"Maddy, this is going to be beautiful, and I know they'll love it. Are you saying I can help you make this, and I can share in creating this?"

She nodded at him, smiling shyly, secretly hoping he would love the idea of them creating together. Belle cooed, looking at the colorful stained-glass panels hanging above her head. *After all*, she thought, *we already created something pretty wonderful together.*

He pulled her into his arms, crushing her against him. He loved this woman who had helped to heal the horrible empty place in him left from the death of his wife and child. He would do anything for her, and making something this special and beautiful, and working side by side with her was something he never thought he would have in his life. He never dreamed he would be married again and have another beautiful child. They couldn't replace what he'd lost. He would always have a special place in his heart for them, but Maddy and Belle were here, were real, and they were his.

"I would love to, Maddy. Thank you."

"Thank you for what?" she asked, her forehead wrinkled. "You're helping me." She looked at him confused.

"No, sweetheart, you're saving me."

⤞

*B*etty's barking pulled their attention to the window looking outside. A young lady was frozen on the path from the driveway to the studio. Betty was trying to happily greet her, but the woman was obviously terrified.

"Betty, come." Jaxx commanded. Immediately the dog turned and flew to Jaxx's side as he and Maddy walked out of the studio through the brightly painted blue Dutch door.

"Thank you," the girl called. "I'm looking for Maddy Grey."

"Hi, I'm Maddy." Maddy walked toward the young woman. Within a few steps they had reached each other and Maddy stretched out her hand and repeated, "I'm Maddy Grey, how can I help you?"

"Hi, I'm Lynn Eric, and my advisor suggested I contact you. Instead of emailing you, I just decided to take a chance and go on a road trip." The auburn-haired beauty suddenly looked unsure of herself, her confidence withering before their eyes. As she paled, her adorable freckles stood out even more against her pale skin. Maddy could tell that the minute the words came out of the girl's mouth all the bravado she had convinced herself she had just slipped away, and now she was stuck in a situation that she wanted to melt away from. Maddy had been there many times and took pity on the girl.

"If you've been driving a while, you're probably thirsty and need a break. Let's go sit on the back porch and have something to drink. Would you like some raspberry iced tea?" She asked kindly.

"I don't want to impose," Lynn said, unsure of how to proceed.

"You're not. I invited you. And this is Jaxx and Belle and Jaxx's dog, Betty"

"Betty? A bull mastiff named Betty?" The girl didn't cover quickly enough before she blurted out what she was thinking. "Seriously?"

"Completely," Jaxx said kindly. "Betty, say hello."

Betty sat in front of Lynn and offered her paw. Delighted, Lynn bent down and took the paw in both her hands.

"I think I'm in love," she proclaimed. "Yes, I would love some raspberry iced tea, and I would love to sit on your porch and look out at that beautiful view." She was beginning to get her nerve back once she realized that Maddy wasn't acting like an arrogant artist. *Maybe this was going to work out okay.*

Once they were settled in the antique metal shell chairs on the back porch, Belle in her play yard with her toys, Maddy looked the girl over. She seemed to have relaxed.

"So, your advisor told you to contact me. I assume you're an art student, you heard about the artist residence program I have here, and you're interested in becoming involved."

"Yes," Lynn turned to look at Maddy. "Everyone is talking about the opportunity you have. Living in a beautiful Victorian house on the beach with studio space in the basement and gallery space in the parlors, plus kilns in a barn and even a forge. Everyone is vying for the opportunity. I imagine your email is full of people applying. I figured I didn't have a snowball's chance in hell unless you met me, so I threw caution to the wind and here I am."

"Not a bad plan," Maddy said, but secretly began worrying about the number of students who might take this same route. Her privacy was important to her and she didn't want this to become a habit. "But maybe you should make it known there is a giant bull mastiff that guards my studio."

Lynn got the message and blushed. Betty thumped her tail against the porch knowing that somehow she was being talked about.

"Yeah, it's a plan that can backfire in a lot of ways," Lynn admitted.

"Actually, you've helped me realize an issue I might have moving forward, so I can thank you for that. So, tell me why I should select you as one of my artists in residence? Why should you get the opportunity over another artist?"

"Because if I don't, I won't ever be an artist," Lynn blurted out, her frustration bubbling to the surface.

"Lynn, living in an old house on the ocean doesn't make you an artist," Maddy said gently. Jaxx sat quietly watching Maddy and Lynn. His instinct told him there was a lot more to Lynn's story. Under the surface there was a slurry of turmoil.

"No, I know that. It's not what I mean. See, I'm a commuter student. I have to live at home to go to school. My parents don't approve of my major. They want me to go into the health care field. There's nothing wrong with being a nurse, but that's not what's in my heart. I can't work at home. My parents criticize me every time I try to do something. I stay at school as long as I can, but since I am still living under my parent's roof, I have to abide by their rules. I get that. It's only fair, but I need a shot to see if I have what it takes. If I don't, I'll change my major. I'll become a nurse and be the best damn nurse that ever walked the earth, but I want the chance to be the best damn artist first." Lynn snapped her mouth shut realizing that she might have just sounded like a crazy woman.

Maddy looked out at the ocean. The girl's impassioned plea moved her. Jaxx reached down and pet Betty, hiding the slight smile tugging at his lips. He knew Maddy. Lynn had touched her heart. Maddy was struggling, trying to be all business-like, but it was all over and Jaxx knew it. He wondered if Lynn did.

Maddy turned the situation over in her head. She grew up with parents who loved art, who dabbled in it and sold their work to tourists in the boutiques up and down the coast. Her creativity was encouraged, and she blossomed. She couldn't imagine what it would have been like to have this dream and not have it nurtured.

"Where are you staying tonight?" Maddy asked.

"I didn't think about it. I will probably drive back tonight."

"If you want, I can take you up to the house. You can spend the night and get a feel for the place. Then we can talk tomorrow morning. How do you feel about that?"

"I don't want to impose..." Lynn said, realizing she had never thought her plan through. She just hopped in her car and headed to Grey's Harbor, a complete impulse move.

"You're not. All of the candidates I consider are invited to spend a night and get a feel for the place before any decision is made."

"Okay, I'll take you up on that. I have to go buy a toothbrush, but sure, I would love to spend a night there."

❧

They finished their tea while making small talk, Maddy getting to know Lynn. She approved of the young lady's manners and her passion for her art. Maddy stood up and collected the glasses asking Lynn if she wanted more before they left.

"No thanks. That was wonderful. Thank you. Can I help in any way?"

"Nope. I'm just going to pop these into the house and grab my keys and we can head over to where you're going to spend the night. I have to close up my studio first though."

Lynn stood, uncertain what to do. Betty walked over to her and leaned against her legs, sensing the woman's stress.

"You can come with us," Maddy assured Lynn as she picked up the sleeping Belle from her play yard, "if Betty will let you go, that is." Lynn laughed as the dog wiggled her butt trying to encourage Lynn to continue petting her.

"Come on, Betty," Jaxx commanded the dog, who obediently fell in step at his master's side as they walked along the dunes to the studio.

Maddy opened the bottom half of the Dutch door and welcomed Lynn into her workspace. Betty was ordered to lay down outside, which she did with a mutter of discontent.

"Oh my gosh! This is beautiful," Lynn gasped as she looked around at the stained-glass panels that hung from the ceiling and the fused glass bowls and plates that filled the shelves that hung on the walls. "I've never had a chance to work in glass. It must be fascinating but scary."

"Scary? You get used to getting cut," Maddy admitted.

"No, not that," Lynn said as she turned around looking at the huge amount of artwork that adorned the space. "I'd be terrified of breaking my material. I think that would be an expensive problem." Lynn wandered over to the partners' desk where the drawing for the wedding arch was still spread out. "This is gorgeous," she said as she studied the design. "Do you weld and work in a forge, too?"

"I've played at the forge, but I'm not talented," Maddy admitted, "and I plan on learning to weld." Maddy glanced over at Jaxx with a smile on her face. "With a little help from my friends."

"Are you going to go to an architectural salvage yard to get some metal pieces for this?" Lynn asked, still not looking up from the sketch.

"Lynn, you're brilliant. I never thought of that, and it might just solve some of my problems." Maddy turned the idea over in her head, realizing that Lynn may have just saved her a lot of time and heartache. An architectural salvage yard might be a treasure chest of old ornate forgings, fence and gate pieces, wall sconces, and shelf and lamp brackets. It could be a perfect solution.

"Thanks," Lynn said, blushing. "I discovered one near my house when I was in high school and was in charge of decorating the gym for prom. We were a small school, and most of the folks didn't have a lot of money. We didn't have proms like the big city schools do. Anyway, I found a bunch of cool stuff that we could use to give the feeling of an estate garden. It's amazing what happens when you stick flowers in architectural elements. Instant garden boutique. We even got a couple of badly damaged porch posts and wound ivy around them. They ended up looking amazing and that's where we had the prom pictures taken."

Lynn's face was lit up with the memory, a wide smile spreading across her face. Maddy was really beginning to like this resourceful young lady and thought she might be a wonderful asset to the artist community she was building at Miss Mirabelle's old home.

10

*M*aeve finished counting the heads of lettuce and made the final check, marking the delivery sheet complete. Breakfast and lunch were done. The specials for the early dinner crowd were prepped and ready to go, and it was time for her to sit down with some hot tea.

Maeve took the corner table near the window and made herself comfortable, her fingers wrapped around the heavy mug. She closed her eyes for a second, just to regroup. She was tired. The morning had been busy, but no more than usual. That would never have made Maeve tired, in fact, she thrived on the fast pace of running her diner. No, this was a different kind of tired. A hopeless kind of tired. A tired she didn't understand and had never felt.

You're depressed, Maeve. The inner voice nagged at her. *No, I'm not. That word is not in my vocabulary,* she argued with herself. She took a deep breath, her eyes still closed, trying to center herself and find peace.

"Hey, Maeve, you okay?"

Maeve opened her eyes to see Maddy smiling down at her, concern written all over her face.

"Yep, just regrouping after a busy morning. Join me?"

"I'd love to. A cup of tea and a cinnamon roll if there are any left," she said to Susie who had appeared like magic at the table.

"Coming right up," Susie replied. "Maeve, can I get you anything?' Susie's eyes didn't miss a trick. Maeve was just not the same since Tank. Even though her relationship with Jeff seemed to be developing nicely, she just wasn't the same.

"No, the tea is enough. Thank you," Maeve said kindly. Susie caught Maddy's eye and shook her head a little. Neither one of them thought that Maeve was doing okay.

"So, what brings you into the diner at this time?" Maeve asked Maddy. "Usually you don't emerge from your studio in the afternoon."

"True. You know me well, but I had an idea I wanted to run past you first. I'm just not sure this is the right time."

"Why not?" Maeve asked, looking at her friend confused.

"Maeve, you're sad. I've known you forever. I know when you're sad. I know when you try to be brave, and I know when you're faking it, trying to convince yourself that everything is okay."

"You don't know me that well," Maeve protested with a smile.

"Bet me. Remember when we were in seventh grade and we borrowed Ryker's scooter? We tried to ride it together and lost control. We hit a tree. You were hurt, but you played it off like it was nothing."

"Yeah, and my arm was broken, but I told you and Ryker that nothing was wrong."

"Yep. That one was easy. Remember when Johnny Macomber died?" Maddy asked softly.

"Yeah," Maeve said, her eyes lost in the past.

"You took care of all of us. We all fell apart when he drowned. Bridger, Tank, and Ryker, and me. We all took it hard. We thought we were all invincible. We were kids and would live forever. Then Johnny and Stan went for the joyride in the boat."

"They were drunk," Maeve said with a sigh.

"Yes, they were. It was an accident waiting to happen. And it did."

Maeve and Maddy both took a sip of their tea, thinking about that time, the hurt, the disbelief.

"The thing is, Maeve, you were there for all of us, but we didn't see that you needed us, too. You were the strong one. You held us together. Remember the night you made spaghetti for all of us and we ate and talked until the next morning?"

"I remember."

"Do you remember barking at me when I tried to help you with the dishes? You told me to go back with the others, that you had this?"

"No," said Maeve honestly.

"Well, you did. You were hurting. Hell, you were actually crying. I could see your reflection in the window above the sink. I left you there because I didn't know what to do. I didn't know how to help you. I let you down."

"No, you didn't Maddy. You've always been a good friend."

"Then let me be a good friend now. Let me help you, because honey, I can see you crying in the reflection in the window."

Maddy reached across the table and took Maeve's hand. Maeve's eyes misted with tears.

"Thanks, Maddy. I love you, and I appreciate it, but I don't know what I need. I think it's just time. I just need time."

"Honey, you can take all the time in the world. You're allowed. And Maeve, you're allowed to date someone without a commitment. You can get to know other men without any strings. That's allowed. And you're allowed to be alone if you want. That's allowed, too." Maddy waited a beat. "And you're also allowed to tell your friend to shut the hell up." She grinned and offered half of her cinnamon roll to Maeve.

Maeve smiled ruefully through unshed tears and snagged the offered roll.

"I'll take you up on that roll, and I won't tell you to shut up. Honestly, Maddy, I needed this today. Thank you. There's something else I need though."

"What's that, honey?'

"I need for everyone to stop tiptoeing around me about Ryker and Jennifer's wedding. I know people are afraid that I'm hurt. Sure, I'm hurt about Tank and me, but I couldn't be happier for my brother and Jennifer, and I want to be a big part of making it magical for them. She asked me to be her Maid of Honor, but I'm afraid she's regretting it because she's afraid of hurting me. How can I make people stop treating me like glass? That is *not* helping me heal."

Maddy looked at Maeve carefully to make sure that the words were speaking the truth.

"Okay, then dive head on into it. I know Jennifer asked you for help picking out her dress. That's about as far as she'll go asking for help. The ball is now in your court. You probably need to make the next move and set a date. We can also throw a girls' get together to help her plan her big day, because honey, she has no idea what to do. Jaxx told me Ryker admitted to him that Jennifer is way out of her element and starting to stress and that's the last thing he wants for her. I think our friend needs help. Are you up for it?"

Maddy watched Maeve's face, the thoughts turning over in her mind. *Maybe this is what Maeve needed to pull her out of a slump. It wasn't her wedding, but it was her brother's and a project she could get her teeth into.* Maddy hoped Maeve would bite. After all, Maeve always put others first.

"Okay, when can you get together?" Maeve asked, straightening up and pulling out her phone glancing at her calendar. "We need to know what kind of *feel* she wants. Is there a theme? What about bridesmaids' dresses? Food? Music?" Maeve's fingers started drumming on the table.

Maddy pulled a notebook and pen out of her satchel and slid it across the table to Maeve. Maeve grinned at her and started making lists.

"What else do you have?" Maeve asked. "I know you didn't just come here to get me out of my slump. You have something else up your sleeve. I know you."

Maddy pulled out a small copy of the drawing of the metal and glass arch and unfolded it in front of Maeve.

"Oh my gosh, Maddy. This is stunning. Are you thinking of them getting married under that on the beach?"

"If they want. Do you think they would want?"

"I know Ryker would, and I am certain Jennifer would. Have you showed them?"

"No, I want it to be a surprise, but I don't want to impose. I'm not too sure how to handle it."

"I've got this for you. It'll be a surprise, but I'll get their permission. Trust me on this one," Maeve said with a conspiratorial smile. Suddenly, Maeve realized Maddy was right. She was hurting. It was okay that she was in pain, and it was okay to share it with a friend, but the best way for Maeve to combat her sadness was to fight back by helping someone else. "Maddy, I am hurting and sad. That's hard for me to say. I am trying to pick up my life, but it's hard. I know that you understand that. When Tripp left you had to feel worse than I do. I made Tank go away. I broke up with him. Tripp left you. How did you survive?"

"I just took one day at a time. And remember, I came and hung with you and my friends. Then, when I least expected it, Jaxx came into my life. Don't force it, honey. Enjoy dating Jeff, but don't force the relationship. In the meantime, fill your world with things to do, and right now, that's planning your brother's wedding."

11

*H*ope poured mimosas into four glasses and made her way out onto the deck. The houseboat rocked gently in the water as a power boat motored by under a slow throttle, heading upriver.

"Those look amazing, Hope," Maeve said as she relieved Hope of two of the mimosas. She handed one to Maddy as Hope handed her second one to Jennifer.

"Thanks, Hope," Jennifer said shyly. 'You didn't have to go to this trouble. The Eggs Benedict look amazing, too."

"Dig in," Hope said, as she took a sip of her drink. "And it's no trouble at all. I love doing this."

"Jennifer, we love you," said Maeve kindly, "and we want your wedding to be everything you hope for. We're here to make that happen for you."

Jennifer's eyes threatened to spill over and she quickly took a sip of her mimosa to cover.

"Okay, I'm not as sappy as the rest of them," Maddy said with a grin, "so let's get down to business. Good Eggs Benedict, by the way, Hope. I think you need to assign us each a job so the burden isn't all on your shoulders. I'd like to volunteer for the ceremony set up."

"Sure, but we're going to be married on the beach..." Jennifer's voice trailed off thinking of all the things she must be forgetting to do.

"Yep, so you're going to need chairs, right? Or is this a quick hit with everyone standing?"

"No, chairs would be good." Jennifer's forehead wrinkled with worry. "What'll we do if it rains? Maybe this is a stupid idea."

Hope reached over and patted her hand, hating the stress on Jennifer's face.

"Honey, have faith, and if it rains, so what? If it's really bad, we can move the ceremony into the marina where the reception's going to be. Problem solved. I think it's a great idea to have Maddy take care of everything on the beach."

"Are you having any kind of flower arrangements or things I need to manage?"

Jennifer dropped her face into her hands, suddenly overwhelmed. This was beyond her.

"Jennifer?" Maeve moved to her side and put her arms around the woman who was going to be her sister-in-law. "It's okay. I think I get what you want. You just want your friends gathered on the beach, surrounding you as you and Ryker promise to love each other. Then you want a casual party at the marina. My guess is dancing under the stars and good food is all you have really thought about."

"Yes, please." Jennifer said, looking miserable.

"Why do you look sad?" Hope asked, wondering what the real issue was. "Are you worried about us going overboard and outside your budget?"

"No, I'm worried about disappointing you guys," she whispered. "You are the best friends I've ever had. Hell, you are the *only* friends I've ever had." She stopped, nervous to go on.

"Keep talking," Maddy said, with mock authority.

"I don't want to hurt anyone's feelings. Look at this. You are so good to me. I just don't know..." She stopped again, at a loss.

"Jennifer, we want what you want. This is your wedding. You can elope if you want. Hell, I'll buy you the ladder. We just want you to be happy, and we want to help you any way you want us to help or butt out any time you need us to back away."

Maddy studied Jennifer's face as she listened to Maeve. It suddenly occurred to Maddy what Jennifer really wanted.

"Jennifer, I'm going to ask you a question, and I want you to be completely honest. I don't want you to worry about imposing or hurting anyone's feelings. I just want the God's honest truth. Okay?"

Jennifer's eyes were large and glistening with tears. She nodded hesitantly.

"Okay, would it make you happy if you gave us a budget and we planned your wedding for you? If we just took the burden off your shoulders and pointed you in the direction to walk?"

Jennifer burst into tears while nodding her head in a vigorous yes.

12

*T*he day dawned clear and sunny with a light breeze and fluffy clouds. It was the perfect day for a wedding. Maddy looked critically at the rows of white chairs set up on the beach facing the ocean.

"Do you think there're enough?" Maddy asked Jaxx, counting them for the umpteenth time.

"No, but there'll never be enough. The entire town will show up on this beach today. This is fine, Maddy. There are enough plus to cover the yes responses to the RSVP. Are you ready to set up the arch?"

"I think so. I'm a nervous about it."

"Don't be. It's beautiful and stable. They're both going to flip when they see it," Jaxx assured her.

Together they carried the metal and glass arch to a space in front of the chairs. Using a rubber mallet, Jaxx drove the legs deep into the sand making certain it wasn't going to go anywhere.

"Hey guys, that looks amazing."

They turned to see Hope walking toward them carrying a large box. Jaxx hurried to take in from her.

"Maddy, I can't believe how beautiful that is." Hope stared at the arch, taking in the fused glass which caught the sunlight, making the blues and greens of the ocean glass glow. Swirls of color framed the edges of the arched panel where sand dollar and starfish glass shapes formed an intricate border. The metal frame that formed the arch completed the design with forged metal pieces repeating the feel of waves. Metal starfish crusted the uprights, and intricate metal sand dollars hung on light chains, dancing in the breeze.

"Do you have the fabric and flowers?" Maddy asked, anxious to see what Hope's vision was to complete design.

"I do. I thought about pulling this gauzy fabric through the back supports so it will move with the breeze but also give a background for the front of the arch. She demonstrated, quickly threading the light white fabric through the metal supports. When she was finished the ends draped gracefully to the sand and swayed in the breeze. Then she pulled out a garland of flowers and threaded them through just in front of the fabric. She stood back and looked at Maddy nervously. After all, it was Maddy's masterpiece, and she didn't want to insult the artist.

"Hope, that's perfect. I had this as a vision for their garden and a place for them to get married under, but I was afraid it wasn't fancy enough for the wedding. Now it is dressed and ready to go. Thank you." She hugged Hope tightly. They smiled at each other knowing that Jennifer was going to have the most amazing day of her life and they got to play a major part in it.

"How's Bridger doing at the marina? Is it ready to go and does he need help?" Jaxx asked Hope.

"I think they're ready. The tables are set up and the caterer is taking care of the linens and stuff. Bridger rented a dance floor and has a million little lights strung up above it, so it should be pretty magical. I think we're ready to go, except we all need to get dressed. What time is Joy doing your hair, Maddy?"

"Oh, in about fifteen minutes, you?"

"Forty-five minutes."

"Don't you guys need to get going or something?" Jaxx said nervously looking at his watch, mystified at the workings of females and weddings.

"Yeah, probably should. You need to spiff it up a bit, too, don't you?" Maddy asked. "Damn, I can't wait to see you in a tux instead of your signature flannel."

"Ryker didn't tell you? We're all wearing flannels." Jaxx laughed and gave Maddy a kiss. "I'll see you in a couple of hours." He took another look at the arch. "I just hope the gulls don't make a mess of this before the wedding."

They all stopped and looked at each other, realization dawning on them.

"Oh crap. What were we thinking?" Maddy looked at Jaxx, expecting a solution. He smiled at her and walked to his truck, pulling out a lightweight, plastic painter's drop cloth and some duct tape.

"We just have to get here early enough to get this down so Jennifer doesn't see a plastic and duct tape monstrosity as a wedding arch!"

They worked together quickly, securing the plastic loosely around the structure. Then the girls scurried off together to get to their appointments with Joy while Jaxx went home to give Betty her walk and get ready for the nuptials.

"*J*ennifer, you look beautiful," Hope gasped as they entered Joyful Cuts. Jennifer turned and smiled shyly at them.

"Joy did an amazing job, didn't she?" she said, looking at herself in the mirror, still not believing her reflection.

"I had a great canvas, honey," Joy said, her hand on her hip, looking critically at her work. "I want something else…"

"What about this?" Hope asked as she pulled a small bag out of her tote.

Joy looked in the bag and her face broke into a large smile. "These are perfect." She didn't ask. Joy didn't bother with that. She always knew what would look good, and her clients always came around to her way of thinking…always.

Working quickly, Joy scattered the small white starfish pins throughout the loose braid that circled Jennifer's head and wove them into the unbound, gently curled hair that cascaded down her back. Joy's thick mane of auburn hair swayed with her movements as she poked and tweaked to her satisfaction. She stood back and checked the overall effect.

"Perfect," she pronounced, sharing the mirror with Jennifer. The contrast was striking. Jennifer, petite and delicate, Joy a fiery redhead with a tattoo of scissors on her forearm and biker boots on her feet. Jennifer lived life carefully, trying to preserve herself, and Joy took it to the edge, daring it to destroy her. Yet, the tough hairdresser worked delicate magic.

She turned to Maddy and appraised her hair. "You're next. What're you thinking?" She had already planned on weaving that Welsh black hair into an intricate Celtic knot in the back with long flowing ends for Maddy, but she was willing to listen.

"Honestly, I don't care. Whatever Jennifer wants," Maddy said, completely unconcerned. She would have thrown it in a ponytail if no one was watching.

"I want whatever Joy does. She makes everything beautiful. Did you see Maeve?" Jennifer said.

"No, where is she?" Hope asked, looking around.

"I'm here," Maeve said as she emerged from the back room with several flutes of champagne. "I think our bride needs a little bubbly for her nerves."

"I know I could use it," Maddy said, reaching for a glass. "You look gorgeous. Can you make me that pretty?" Maddy asked Joy.

"I can make you your own pretty. That's what I do," she said, not unkindly. "Hop up in the chair." Joy waited while Maddy got settled but watched Hope the whole time. She needed to think about Hope because she would be doing her bridal hair next spring.

In minutes Maddy's thick dark tresses were trained into three intricate Celtic knots woven down the back of her head laying over the rest of her free-flowing hair.

"Yes?" Joy asked, her eyebrows raised as she held a mirror so Maddy could see the back of her head.

"Oh, yes," replied Maddy, remembering the portrait of Madeline

Abuchon that hung in the historical society. She was now the spitting image of her historic namesake.

"Then head on over to Chrissy so she can do your makeup. You don't want me doing that shit. Okay, Hope, you're up."

Jen looked at Hope critically until Hope started to squirm under her gaze.

"What's wrong?" Hope asked, wondering what the problem was.

"Are you still getting married on a boat or did you decide on the Methodist church?"

"The church because we were afraid our guests might get seasick. Why?"

"Because we can't do the same hair."

"I'm thinking more formal for my own wedding," Hope said, nervous she was giving Joy directions. Joy smiled. She liked that power.

"Like this?" She gathered Hope's hair and twisted in quickly in a low S on the nape of her neck, sleek and sophisticated.

"Yes, like that. Sophisticated but not severe," Hope agreed.

"Then I'm going to do a side braid with some soft curls framing your face for today." She didn't wait for approval. It wasn't a question up for discussion, and Hope was certain she was in good hands. She glanced over at Maddy, where Chrissy was putting on the finishing touches of makeup. She had never seen Maddy look more beautiful.

In a few minutes, Joy was done with Hope, and the result was soft, romantic, and stunning. It was perfect for the beach wedding.

"Now, you guys are okay for a little bit while I get myself all gussied up, right? Make yourself at home in the back room. I think Chrissy has a steamer back there if anyone needs it." She shooed them into the back and picked up a curling iron. A few quick turns in her thick auburn hair were enough to satisfy her that she was fancy enough for the wedding of her good friend, Ryker.

She'd thought about dating him once, but he'd been enamored with Margot, and Joy didn't feel like competing with a socialite. If that's what turned Ryker's head, he wasn't for her. A good friend? Yes. A lover? No.

These girls in her shop had snagged themselves some good men. Jaxx was interesting. Maddy had him wrapped around her finger, but he was the kind of guy who was not intimidated by women who rode Harley's. It was too bad he was taken. Joy glanced down at her favorite motorcycle boots. She hated to have to change those for the wedding, but there were some things you just had to do. Jaxx would have been a very good catch...

Maeve popped her head around the corner, holding a dress hung carefully on a hanger. It was a soft blue-green, the color of water in the Bahamas. One shoulder had a flat, wide strap that held up the bodice which looked like it would hug the body nicely as it dropped into a soft, draping skirt. The other shoulder would be bare.

"Is this your dress?" Maeve asked, admiring it.

"Yeah," Joy said, adding a touch of spray to her hair. "Why? No good?"

"Ah, no. I think it is very good. I can't wait to see it on you." Maeve turned and walked back into the back room, the wispy, cornflower blue bridesmaid dress dancing around her ankles, kissing the top of her pearl encrusted sandals.

Joy suddenly remembered that Maeve and Tank were no longer an item. She was dating that frat boy type, Jeff. Tank was one good looking guy, and a decent person, but they were volatile in the same room. They pushed each other's buttons on purpose, just to enjoy the fireworks. She would have to remember to behave herself today. This was Jennifer's day. Jennifer Creely, the girl whose daddy beat her up regularly and everyone pretended not to notice because it was too uncomfortable to confront the issue. Luckily, Jennifer made it out the other side, and Joy was certain her old man was rotting in hell. It was too bad about Maeve and Tank. That Jeff guy was nice, but Tank and Maeve belonged together. Joy sighed as she unlaced her boots. It was also too bad she didn't have a date. She wasn't fond of being on the prowl at weddings. Sometimes mistakes were made when that happened.

"Wait, you're not going like that," Chrissy said as she pushed Joy's shoulders until she was seated in the salon chair. "I have some work to do on you." She picked up a make-up brush and went to work while Joy watched her with mock distrust.

"Do *not* make me look like a cheap hooker down on Dock Street," Joy warned, knowing full well Chrissy would never do that.

"*A*re you ready, sweetie?" Maeve asked, looking down at Jennifer, who was radiant, but visibly nervous.

"I am. I just want to get this going."

"Then let's do it. The girls all have their bouquets, and they're gorgeous. I'll hand you yours after you get out of the Surrey at the ceremony. Bridger called Hope and your guests are seated, so let's get this show on the road.

Hope and Maddy walked out of the shop, holding the door for Maeve and Jennifer. Maeve held up Jennifer's short, wispy train so it wouldn't drag in the street.

Johnny Rayburn grinned and tipped his hat as he helped Jennifer and Maeve get seated in the bicycle powered Surrey, it's jaunty red and white striped awning and white fringe making it the perfect beach conveyance vehicle. Greg Watson did the same for Maddy and Hope.

"Ready?" Johnny called out.

"Yep. Thanks, guys," Jennifer replied, giddy with nerves.

The boys cycled down Main Street heading for the wooden ramp sidewalk that led down to the beach. Well-wishers waved and called good luck as the little parade passed by.

Within minutes, they were moving down the wooden walkway, and Jennifer gasped at the crowd. The seats were filled with her invited guests, but it looked like the rest of the town lined the dunes of the beach all wanting to witness the nuptials of Ryker Wynn and Jennifer Creely.

For a minute, Jennifer felt like bolting. This was way too much. There were too many people. Maeve lay a hand on her thigh and patted it.

"You've got this. All these people love you and Ryker. They're here because they're happy for you and want to support you. Relax and enjoy."

"Oh my... Where did that...It's beautiful. Maddy, you did that didn't you?" Jennifer turned and looked into the Surrey next to her. Maddy was looking critically at the arch, seeing the way the sun filtered through the glass, looking at the fabric swaying in the breeze. She pulled her eyes from it and looked at Jennifer.

"I hope it's okay," she said, noticing the tears in Jennifer's eyes.

"Okay? It's so beautiful. I can't believe you did that for Ryker and me. I've never seen anything like it. Thank you for letting us use it."

"Use it? Honey, it's yours if you want it. You can take it home for your garden or trash it. It's all yours." Maddy was touched at the raw emotion on her friend's face. Jennifer just didn't get how much they all loved her.

"Wipe your tears," Maeve counseled. "It's time."

Greg helped Maddy and Hope out of their Surrey and they lined up ready to walk through the break in the dunes and down the sand aisle to the arch. Each carried a small gathering of flowers tied together with ribbons the color of the sea.

Maeve got out of the Surrey, and with Johnny's help, extracted Jennifer and her dress, keeping everything intact. Then Maeve reached into the box in the back and pulled out Jennifer's bouquet, an armload of flowers tied together with braided ribbons which hung down toward the ground, the ribbons adorned with starfish and sand dollars.

The string quartet began to play, Izzy bent over her cello so no one could see the tears glistening in her eyes, and Maddy then Hope began the processional. A small voice called out as Maddy passed by the front row of chairs.

"Mama." Belle waved her hand at her mommy and the people around her smiled indulgently at the beautiful child.

As Hope walked toward the arch her heart skipped a beat when she saw Bridger standing up there as one of Ryker's groomsman. She would be making this walk next year, only then it would be to make her vows to the man who was smiling at her, thinking the same kinds of thoughts. Suddenly, she wondered if a long engagement was such a good idea. She wished they were starting their life together today, too.

Bridger just grinned at her, reading her mind. He winked as she turned and made her way to her spot next to the arch. She focused on Maeve who was halfway up the aisle. Maeve's eyes were misted, and it wasn't hard to see that Tank's were, too. Hope's heart broke a little realizing the toll this was taking on her friends. She watched as Maeve cast her eyes down as she turned away from Tank to take her place and wait for the bride. Tank's eyes never left Maeve's face.

The music changed and there was a collective gasp as Jennifer stepped from behind the Surrey and started her walk down the aisle.

"Damn, Ryker," Tank whispered. "She's beautiful."

"I know," Ryker tried to say, but a lump of emotion was caught in his throat.

Jennifer's dress, a slim fitting illusion bodice encrusted with lace, pearls and starfish emphasized her narrow waist before it flared out into a mermaid tulip train scattered with starfish, pearls, and rhinestones that flashed in the sun. As she made her way up the aisle her eyes never wavered from the hold that Ryker's had on hers. Her nerves slipped away, and a smile tugged at her lips. She was the epitome of the blushing bride, and she charmed each guest as she made her way past them, the love for the man she was about to marry obvious on her face.

He reached for her as she walked to him and he had to stop himself from embracing her then and there.

"Oh, God, you are so beautiful." He thought he said it quietly, but the ocean breeze carried the words to everyone, and the well-wishers laughed with delight.

Reverend Abernathy opened the ceremony and welcomed Grey's Harbor to the promises of Ryker and Jennifer.

"*H*ey, Maeve," said Tank as he walked up and stood beside her watching Ryker and Jennifer dancing under the twinkling lights.

"Hey, Tank." Maeve, her eyes on the newlyweds, had a sad smile on her face.

"We did good," Tank stated, looking down at her, shocked at her sadness.

"We did good what?" she said, sighing.

"We did good at Best Man and Maid of Honor," he replied, raising his champagne glass in salute.

"You're right, Tank. We did do good at that." She glanced at him, but just for a moment, knowing her eyes were going to fill with tears.

"Maeve…" he began.

"Hey, pretty lady, are you ready to dance with me?" Jeff slid an arm around her waist, leading her to the dance floor. She glanced over her shoulder back at Tank. He didn't miss the fact that her eyes were unusually bright with unshed tears.

"Tank," Bridger said as he came up behind his friend.

"What Bridger?"

"You're a damn idiot." Bridger took a swig of his beer.

"I can't argue with that." Tank replied. "I really can't."

13

*T*ank and Jaxx stepped into the Mizzen Mast. It had been a rough day at work, and they agreed that some Sperm Whale Ale would be good for the soul.

"Hey guys, why don't you belly up to the bar tonight," Izzy advised.

"We were thinking of heading out to the deck," Tank said with a little wave toward the back door.

"I'm lonely and you guys can keep me company," Izzy retorted.

"Let me guess," Tank said, "Maeve and Jeff are out there."

Jaxx led the way to a couple of stools at the bar and Tank followed.

"They are, but that's not why I wanted you to sit at the bar with me. Truthfully, I wouldn't mind the company tonight."

"You okay, Iz?"

"Yeah, it's just one of those nights. It's not a bad idea to have to friends around. What can I get you?"

"Sperm Whale for us," Tank said giving Izzy a one-armed hug before she moved behind the bar. "So, Maeve and Jeff are becoming quite the item, aren't they?"

"Yeah, but you know that."

"What's the talk?"

"You mean do I have inside information about their relationship."

She cocked her head looking Tank hard in the eyes. Jaxx looked up finding the antique ceiling tins suddenly incredibly interesting. "I might, but I wouldn't share it with you."

Tank groaned and took a swig of the beer Izzy opened and handed him.

"I'll tell you this, my friend."

"What's that, Izzy?"

"You're an idiot."

Jaxx snorted and took a swig of his beer.

"Right as usual, Izzy," Tank agreed.

"So, what are you going to do about it? When are you going to use the brains the good Lord gave you?"

"It's too late, Izzy. The damage is done. Besides, Maeve is better off with Jeff."

"What the hell are you talking about? Jaxx, what's with this guy?"

Jaxx just shrugged and raised the bottle to his lips, disengaging from the conversation.

"Izzy, I'm just a carpenter. I don't have anything to offer Maeve. Jeff is a successful architect who lives on the north end. He can offer Maeve the world."

"Maeve doesn't want the world, Tank. Hi, Jaxx, Izzy." Maddy hugged them all and slid onto a barstool next to Jaxx. "If you think that Maeve cares about that stuff, you never really knew her, Tank, and that's probably the biggest problem right there. You could change the course of all this if you wanted."

"I want her to be happy and cared for. I don't want her to want for anything. Jeff can give her that."

"But can he give her the love she wants?" asked Izzy wisely.

Izzy, Maddy, and Jaxx looked at Tank who just grumbled and excused himself to the men's room.

"He's his own worst enemy," Jaxx said.

"And he's an idiot," Maddy observed.

They all raised their glass to that sentiment.

"Come with me," Jeff insisted. He was holding both of Maeve's hands in his, smiling at her indecision. "It'll be fun. I only have to meet with my client on one day, and it'll only be a couple of hours in the morning. You can laze away in bed, enjoying a late morning at the hotel, or you can go shopping, or whatever Maeve does when she has time to herself."

He knew it was going to be a tough sell, but Maeve needed a break. Planning and executing Jennifer's wedding was a labor of love for Maeve but doing that and running the restaurant had left its mark. She looked pale and drawn, not like the woman he had started dating a month or so ago.

"I'd love to, Jeff, but I can't leave the restaurant. Who'd run it?"

"You have Pete and Susie. They've taken care of it before when you haven't been there."

"I've only left for a couple of hours during the day, and not during the morning or lunch rush. I've never been gone for three days." She protested. She felt badly because she knew he really wanted her with him, and he wanted to do something special for her. But she really couldn't leave. No one else knew what needed to be ordered and when. No one else came in and started the prep work. It was her business, and she was the only one who knew the intricacies.

"Maeve, that's not how to run a business." He smiled as he watched her back stiffen. She didn't welcome the criticism. "What if you needed to go out of town for a family emergency or something?"

"The only family I have is here in Grey's Harbor."

"Attend a friend's wedding?"

"The only friends that count are here in Grey's."

"What if, God forbid, you got sick?" He was serious. That could ruin a business if no one else could step in.

"I don't," she answered mildly, clearly done with the conversation.

He looked at the drawn face and thought otherwise, but he tried another tactic.

"You can tell a successful, well-run business by its ability to run smoothly while the management attends to other things." It was a challenge and he knew it. He also figured she would rise to the bait.

"My business is successful and well-run. If necessary, I could have everything arranged so I could be absent. I am organized enough for that to happen if need be." She took a sip of her Crab Pot Porter and looked out over the river, thinking about her brother and the new home he was making with Jennifer at the cabin down the river a ways. She was happy for them. She had never seen her brother so content. She sighed.

"So then it's settled. You're a good enough businesswoman that you can come away with me for a couple days. Maeve, you need the break."

"Here's your loaded potato soup and patty melt, Jeff. Maeve, your soup. Are you sure you don't want anything else, honey?" Izzy asked, carefully looking at her friend, taking in the pale skin and dark circles under her eyes.

"No, thank you, Izzy. This is good." Maeve smiled at Izzy and reached for the soup spoon nestled next to the large bowl in front of her. "It smells heavenly."

"Thanks," said Izzy. "It should. It's your recipe after all." They both laughed remembering the day years ago they worked side by side to create the perfect bowl of potato soup. Once they agreed they had achieved greatness, they also agreed they would both serve it in in their own establishments, the only difference was the garnish. Izzy smothered it in bacon, cheese, and scallions, where Maeve's was garnished with chunks of lobster.

"Okay," said Izzy, "Just let me know if you need anything else." She glanced at Jeff and he nodded his thanks.

When Izzy slid back behind the bar, Jaxx called for another round. When she put it down in front of them Maddy spoke in a quiet voice.

"Izzy, what's wrong?"

"What's wrong with what?"

"I know you well enough to know when something's up, so spill it."

"I can leave," Jaxx offered and he looked around, spotting Tank standing at a table talking to some friends.

"No need," Izzy said with a sigh. "Thanks, Maddy. I'm just having one of those days. I've got a lot on my mind and having friends around makes things easier. I'm glad you stopped by. I'm fine. Not gonna fall off the wagon or anything, but still, it's good to have you here. More than anything right now, I'm worried about Maeve."

"I know," said Maddy. "She just hasn't been herself lately."

"She doesn't look well. Maeve always had a feisty spark in her eyes. I feel like it's dead."

"Yeah. Jeff's a great guy. There's no denying that, but he doesn't bring a smile to her eyes."

"She's wounded. You can't see the damage, there's no open cut, but she's bleeding out just the same. Pretty soon, she'll bleed dry," Jaxx mused as he took a sip of his beer.

"You know about that kind of wound, don't you," Izzy said, watching him. Jaxx rarely spoke about his personal life.

"When my wife and child were killed, I died with them. I walked around and functioned. I did my job, but I was dead inside."

"Maddy changed that," Izzy said, glancing at the girl sitting next to him, knowing that under the bar, Maddy's hand rested somewhere on Jaxx, connecting with him.

"Well, Betty first," said Jaxx, lightening up the moment, "but Maddy helped some." He grinned at Maddy as she swatted him lightly. It felt good to be able to joke, to smile. It was good to feel he wasn't dishonoring his wife and little girl just because he was happy again, in love again. In fact, he was pretty sure they approved of the way his life was now going. He wasn't a sentimental man, far from it, but he was glad he found his way to Grey's Harbor and to Maddy Grey.

Tank came back to the bar and settled on the stool again next to Jaxx

"What are you all talking about all serious like?"

"Nothing special. Just the current thinking around Grey's Harbor that you're daft," Izzy said with a grin. "And if you don't figure things out really soon, you're going to lose big time." Tank followed her eyes to see Maeve and Jeff leaving the bar, hand in hand. They all overheard Jeff's jubilant words.

"I can't believe I won! We'll have a great time in Nag's Head." He held the door for Maeve, and as he did, he caught sight of the group at the bar watching him. He saluted them, a triumphant smile on his face.

"I'd say the game it over," Tank growled as he drained his beer.

"No, my friend, it's not. If you'd stand up and be half the man I know you to be, you would get in there and fight. This is just a skirmish," Izzy retorted.

Tank glared at her, his mind jumbled, wanting his girl back, but wanting what was best for her.

"Tank, only you can decide. Wars are won and lost all the time. There are casualties on the battlefield and casualties at home. When the innocent die, it's the worst causality of all. The unfortunate part is, often wars are fought for the wrong reason. I'd make sure you're surrendering for the right reason and the innocent don't suffer the consequences of your actions." Jaxx let that sink in for a minute. "Now, who would like to thoroughly trounce me in a game of darts," he offered innocently, knowing he could probably beat them all blindfolded.

14

*M*aeve leaned her head back against the headrest, her eyes closed. Her hair lifted in the breeze as they sped along the coast, the top down in Jeff's blue BMW Z-4. He looked over and smiled. She actually looked like she might be starting to relax.

It had been a rough start to the trip. She fussed over the order that was supposed to arrive, going over the list with Pete until Jeff thought Pete just might bury a meat cleaver in her skull.

Susie looked like she was ready to scream and drag Maeve out by her hair, but she and Pete understood that this was hard for their boss. It wasn't that she didn't trust them. It was just that she couldn't let go of the Cathead. It was her child, and no one was good enough to take care of it. Susie had joked about installing a nanny cam so Maeve could watch them. The joke fell flat when they realized that Maeve was turning the idea over in her head.

After they had gone over the instructions for the umpteenth time, Jeff finally managed to drag her out of the restaurant to the applause of diners who were a witness to the struggle. Promises were made and the door finally shut on Maeve as she and Jeff made their way to his car. What Maeve didn't see was Pete and Susie collapse into a booth in feigned exhaustion from having to deal with their boss, much to the delight of the clientele.

Now they were well on their way. They would check into the hotel and enjoy some time on the beach. Then Jeff planned on wining and dining her in the evening, followed by a long night of lovemaking. He would meet with his client in the morning, then spend the day with Maeve playing tourist and sightseeing all the cheesy stuff people from the mid-west would visit on a family vacation. After another night of worshipping Maeve, they would return home. He was hoping she would feel rested and loved and the color and light would return to her face.

Maeve's mind was racing. She knew Jeff was watching her, aching to see her relax and enjoy herself. She didn't want to disappoint him. He was trying so hard, but leaving the diner felt like she had just cut another tie to her life. First Tank, and now, leaving the diner…It was only for a few days, but it was the wrong time. Jeff just didn't get that. The problem was, Jeff didn't get her.

Of course, she didn't get her.

Maeve was miserable. She knew the situation was of her own making. She had pushed Tank away. She wanted to get on with her life. She wanted a husband and a family, and Tank wasn't ready to make that happen. Now she had Jeff, a wonderful man with an amazing future who obviously worshipped her. Why couldn't she be happy with that? She was such a bitch, but she felt like she was living a lie.

It's not like she had told him she loved him. She didn't make him any promises or commitments. She had just enjoyed her time with him, but she knew he was looking for more. It was almost like his biological clock was ticking. Sometimes she thought his interest in her was more business, that she would be an asset to him socially, but he never paraded her around. This was the first time he had ever asked her along for any of his business appointments, and she wasn't meeting his client. She was just along for the ride.

Stop it, she told herself. *You need to stop overthinking and just enjoy having someone interested in you. Just stop being a bitch.* She opened her eyes and looked at Jeff. He sensed her and glanced at her, taking his eyes off the road for a second.

"What?" he asked, smiling.

"This is nice. I like having the top down." She shook her hair, feeling the freeness of the open car.

"Good. I want you to just enjoy. We'll be at the hotel in about half an hour, then we'll have some lunch. Sound good?"

"Sounds wonderful."

They pulled into a small, but beautiful seaside hotel and quickly checked in. As she put away her suitcase and placed her toiletries case in the bathroom, she couldn't help but glance at the bed, understanding where this was going to lead.

Of course it wouldn't the first time for them. They were developing a healthy intimate relationship, but, if she were to be totally honest with herself, she was never really 'there' for the experience, always holding herself back, not committed, not involved. It made her feel horrible, and a little sick to her soul. Actually, it might be eating her alive. She stopped herself from sighing, realizing she did that often, and arranged a smile on her face.

"I love this door leading out to the patio on the beach. The ocean breeze is going to feel amazing tonight."

Jeff frowned, realizing she meant to leave the sliding door open as they slept, with only the screen to close out the world. He wasn't sure how he felt about that.

"I'm thinking of some crab cakes for lunch. How does that sound?" Jeff asked, coming up behind Maeve, his arms around her, drawing her close.

"Sounds delicious," she said trying hard to enjoy his lips against the back of her neck. He turned her toward him and looked into her eyes, his questioning, hers hooded. "Are you okay, honey?"

"Absolutely," she replied. She wasn't lying. She was fine. This was her new normal. She knew what she had lost, but that didn't mean she couldn't learn to love this man. He was good and kind and attentive. He was skilled at lovemaking, and he worked to make her feel special. She was so unfair to him.

She pulled his face to hers and kissed him deeply, convincingly. She worked at letting her soul go and connecting with this wonderful person. She felt her spirits lift a little. He felt it and responded. There was no denying she was becoming aroused. Maybe, with a little more work, this relationship had a future.

O nce Maeve decided to let go, the next two days were enjoyable for both of them. She slept in, something she never got to do, while Jeff met with his client. The meeting went well, and Jeff was ecstatic. To celebrate they shopped with abandon and booked a dinner cruise, toasting the night away with champagne.

When they got back to the hotel room, they were both in high spirits and feeling no pain. With the ocean breeze caressing their skin, they made love until the wee hours of the morning.

The ride back home was comfortably quiet and relaxed. The stress lines had melted from Maeve's forehead and a smile played at the corners of her mouth. Jeff was happy to see the change in her, and he felt that he was responsible for the shift. The weekend had been a success, both for his business prospects and his personal prospects, although they weren't mutually exclusive.

15

"I should be there in about fifteen minutes," Jaxx said, his phone on speaker in the truck.

"Where are Ryker and Tank?" Maddy asked, trying to figure how long it would be before they all showed up at her house. She had invited everyone to a bonfire on the beach to welcome Ryker and Jennifer back from their honeymoon.

"About five or ten minutes behind me." He concentrated on the road ahead. Something didn't look right.

"Jaxx, what's wrong?" Maddy picked up in the shift of his tone.

"An accident, I think. Honey, I'll call you back." He slowed the truck, his brain assessing what he was seeing. It was a lonely stretch of the road the locals used when they wanted to avoid the freeway, or they liked a scenic winding drive along the river.

It was an accident, and it was bad. He pulled over to the side of the road, slamming the truck into park. Jumping out, he hurried to the tangled mass of steel a few yards in front of him.

His heart started to pound, sweat breaking out on his forehead. This was bad. Very bad. One vehicle was on its roof in the middle of the road, a body ejected in front. He reached that first. His training kicked in. It only took a glance to recognize that the body in front of him was beyond help. He moved on to the second car.

Vaguely familiar.

He reached the vehicle

There was blood.

Everywhere.

Long blonde hair covered in blood.

Skin flayed back, the white cheekbone visible.

Choppers. Did he hear choppers? *Gunfire. Get down.*

He shook his head. He needed to stay clear.

Screaming. There was screaming filling his ears, confusing his brain.

"Maeve!"

The sound of footsteps running toward him.

The enemy?

He shielded the body. He needed to protect the dignity of the body from the enemy. He needed to protect her.

"Maeve. Oh, God, Maeve."

"Get back!" Jaxx snarled as he reached into the car placing two fingers on her carotid, checking for a pulse.

"Get out of my way!" Tank yelled, grabbing for the back of Jaxx's shirt.

"Stand down solider," Jaxx commanded, loudly, not to be disobeyed. "I need a medic," he shouted. "Medic!"

With a roar, Tank shoved Jaxx aside and ripped the door open, sheer animal strength doing the impossible.

"I need a fucking medic!" Jaxx yelled, looking around for the familiar red cross on a bag coming his way. "Damn it, soldier, radio a medic."

Tank leaned in the car, trying to make sense of what he was seeing. Maeve's beautiful face destroyed, a turn signal lever sticking out of her shoulder, and blood, so much blood.

"Maeve, honey, don't leave me. Please, God, don't let her die. I love her. Maeve, I love you. Please, wake up Maeve." Sheer anguish filled Tank's voice as he begged God for help. He wanted to touch her but was terrified of causing more damage. His hands were covered in blood.

So much blood.

"If you're not going to get out of the way apply pressure here," Jaxx commanded, grabbing Tank's two fingers and pushing down hard on the femoral artery. Vivid images, memories of the war, of Greg slammed Jaxx, the arterial bleed pumping, spraying blood, draining the life out of his best friend.

"I just called 911," a disembodied female voice said shakily. "Oh, God!"

"Get back," Jaxx commanded. "Look for other casualties." *It was always good to give the soldiers a job. It kept their mind off the dying.* He heard moaning and he looked to Maeve, *was she actually coming around?* No, it was behind him. He turned and glanced back. It was Ryker. That brought him back to his senses. This was Ryker's sister. This was Tank's girl. She was not going to die. He would not let that happen.

He tore his shirt off and rolled it into a collar, slipping it under her chin. The seat belt was tight against her throat, and he realized the faint gurgling he heard came from the belt pushing hard against her throat, or maybe she couldn't breathe because her face was collapsed. He pulled his knife from his pocket and made quick work of the seatbelt, making certain Maeve's position didn't shift when it snaked free.

Blood sprayed upward, blinding him for a minute.

"Press harder, damn it! Press with everything you've got," he ordered Tank.

"I don't want to hurt her. I can't hurt her," Tank cried, tears falling unchecked down his face.

"If you don't push that artery hard against her bone, she will die!" Jaxx said, knowing that the cold hard facts would be enough to kick Tank's fight into gear. Jaxx grabbed Tank's fingers and guided them into the gore, showing him just where to push. He had lost track of Ryker. He couldn't be bothered with that right now.

Choppers. Sirens. He heard choppers again. He started to shake. He had to stay present, to help Maeve. There weren't any gunshots, so his soldiers were safe. *Stay present*. The chopper landed. People were running. Medics.

"Move out of the way." It was a command. He was trained to follow commands.

"Arterial bleeding. Femoral artery," Jaxx reported. "Object penetration to right shoulder, severe facial laceration...." He rattled off his observations as the EMS workers rendered aid to Maeve. They worked quickly, packing the wound with clot dressing and applying a tourniquet to her mangled thigh, then taping the shift lever to her shoulder so it wouldn't dislodge. When they intubated her Tank groaned.

"Maeve, oh God, honey. I'm sorry. I'm so sorry."

A few minutes later, Maeve was on a backboard, and the crew was moving her toward the waiting helicopter.

Jaxx and Tank followed them in shock themselves. Walking zombies.

"You can't come with us."

"Bullshit," roared Tank.

"We don't have time to argue with you. Talk to your friend," the medic said to Jaxx as he secured Maeve in the chopper and they lifted her to the sky.

He needed to take charge. His ears were thrumming, the chopper taking off. He was listening for gunfire. He needed to take a head-count. Greg was dead. He knew that. He wasn't sure where Charlie was. *No wait, not Charlie, Ryker. It was Ryker and Tank here. You're in Grey's Harbor, and you needed to take charge. Stay present.*

Bridger Cadigan pulled his truck off to the side of the road. Izzy had called him. She always knew shit before anyone else. *God, what was he going to do?* Hope reached over and took his hand, squeezing it, giving him strength.

"We have to help our friends. Come on," she said. She climbed out of the truck and moved forward. A policeman stopped her shaking his head.

"You can't come any closer, ma'am."

"Those are our friends standing there," Bridger said. "We've come to drive them to the hospital."

"Which ones?" the officer asked.

"All of them," Bridger replied as he walked past the officer and intercepted Tank trying to get into the driver's side of Ryker's truck. "Tank, I'll drive you to the hospital. I've got Hope here, too. We can get you, Ryker, and Jaxx to the hospital."

Hope came up behind Tank and slid a blanket around his shoulders. He didn't notice, his eyes red with anger and disbelief.

"Tank, honey, get in the passenger side. I'm going to get Ryker."

Bridger took the keys from Tank's hand, wondering how he got them from Ryker. He would sort that out later.

Hope found Ryker standing next to Maeve's car, staring at the driver's seat. She tried not to look, didn't want to see the damage, but her nose was filled with the smell of blood. *Maeve.* Hope's eyes filled with tears. *Maeve.*

She gently put another blanket around Ryker's shoulders, nodding thanks to the paramedic who had provided it. She put her arms around Ryker and led him away. He didn't say a word. He just stumbled next to her.

"Jaxx, are you okay?" she asked as he looked up at her from where he stood near an ambulance. A paramedic had been talking to him.

"Yeah, thanks, Hope. I'm fine. Go on. Get Ryker to the hospital."

Hope nodded and led Ryker to Bridger's truck.

"You're not fine, sir. I know what happened to you, soldier. You need to debrief." The paramedic was sympathetic but firm. He had been there. Done that.

"You're right, but right now I need to get to the hospital. I'm together, I'm present, and I am functioning fully," he assured the man. The thrumming in his ears had stopped. The sweat had dried, and he was exhausted from the adrenaline surge, but for the time being, he was fine. He had no doubt he was going to be revisiting this, and probably at an inopportune moment.

His phone rang. His truck. He walked over to it as Hope pulled away with Ryker, following Bridger and Tank.

"Hello?" His voice sounded off. Even he recognized that fact.

"Jaxx, honey, are you okay?" It was Maddy. His Maddy. Tears filled his eyes. *Maeve.*

"I'm okay. Maeve…"

"How bad. I heard there was an accident. How bad is it, Jaxx?"

He could hear the hysteria rising in her voice.

"Shhhh, honey." He ached to be there with her. To comfort her. He needed to protect her. He tried to protect Maeve. To help her. To save her. His heart rate elevated.

"You need Betty, don't you," Maddy said, realizing the toll this was taking on Jaxx.

"I'm okay," he repeated. He had to keep it together. *Stay present. For Maddy. For Tank and Ryker.*

"Are you going to the hospital? Maeve is at the hospital, right? She's going to be okay, right?" Again, the edge of panic creeping into her voice.

"I'm going to pick you up and we'll go together," he decided, speaking firmly.

"And we'll bring Betty," Maddy said, just as firmly. She had a feeling Jaxx was going to need his dog.

"*W*here's Belle?" Jaxx asked Maddy as he came through the door. He didn't wait for an answer but gathered Maddy into his arms holding her tight to his chest. She was everything that was good and right in his life. Maddy and Belle. He buried his nose in her hair, breathing deeply her sweet scent, trying to erase the metallic smell of blood.

Blood.

He was covered in blood, and now he had contaminated Maddy. He pulled back suddenly. Betty whined and leaned against his legs, a solid real force of love.

"What's wrong, why did you pull back?"

"Honey, I'm covered in blood. I'm afraid I got it on you." He looked at her shirt, becoming frantic with the thought of Maddy covered in blood, too.

Betty put a paw up on Jaxx's thigh and woofed softly, drawing his attention to her. He looked down at her, meeting her eyes. She reared up gently, putting both paws on his shoulders. She licked his face carefully. Then sat in front of him, watching.

He calmed.

"Jaxx, I'm fine. It's Maeve's blood. She is us. We are fine. Let's go.

"Belle?"

"She's with Mary and Henry. They'll take care of her as long as necessary. You know she has everything she could possibly need at the big house."

Maddy picked up an insulated tote bag and gently ushered Jaxx out the door. It was going to be a long night.

Jaxx opened the passenger door and only then realized Maddy was carrying the heavy tote. He kicked himself for not taking it from her and carrying it himself. He wasn't as present as he thought. Again, Betty whined.

"Jaxx, honey, I'm pulling rank on you. Please give me the truck keys." Without a word he handed them over to her and climbed into the back seat of the truck, Betty joining him, settling half on the seat and half on his lap. Jaxx rested a hand on the big dog's head and started to pet her, slowly, rhythmically, breathing in and out. The dog leaned into her master, giving him comfort and energy. Giving him peace.

Maddy watched them in the rearview mirror. She knew Jaxx suffered PTSD. He never talked about it. She only ever saw brief moments and usually only after Betty moved to her master and leaned her bulk against his legs, bringing him into the present. Maddy had never seen this before. The vacant look in Jaxx's eyes. The stress lines on his face. Jaxx was always the strong one, in charge and in control. It broke her heart to see him this way because she knew what this had to be doing to him. She knew it would make him feel less like the man he should be. She wouldn't let that happen.

She drove carefully to the hospital. She struck up a one-sided conversation with Jaxx and Betty, telling them what projects she was working on in the studio today. Telling Jaxx about Belle's attempt to butter her own waffles this morning and how it resulted in the second bath of the day.

She kept up the light banter, not expecting any return conversation, until she heard a voice from the back. It was strained, but it was present.

"I love you, Maddy."

"I love you, too, Jaxx. Forever and always."

"Forever and always," he repeated.

He sat up straighter and Betty lifted her head from his lap and looked around.

"I didn't bring her vest," Jaxx said, worry setting in again. Betty pushed against him.

"Jaxx, I have it. We're good." She glanced in the mirror again. She saw him visibly relax.

They finally reached the hospital and Maddy parked in a spot out of the way of the emergency entrance. She wanted to give Jaxx a few seconds to gather himself before they entered the hospital. She got out and opened the back door for Betty and Jaxx. Betty unwound herself from her master and jumped out, turning to watch Jaxx, both Maddy and Betty wanting to be sure he was present.

He was.

His eyes were clear, and his jaw was set. He was ready to help his friends, whatever it took.

"Did you need this bag?" he asked, picking up the heavy tote.

"I do. It's filled with drinks, sandwiches, and snacks. I think it's going to be a very long night."

"You're such a good person, Maddy." He hugged her briefly then watched while she fastened Betty's service dog vest on her. Betty's demeanor shifted. She was in public and on the job. She would be on her very best behavior.

The three of them walked into the emergency room exit. A security guard started to say something about Betty but noticed her vest and just nodded as they passed through the doors.

*H*ope saw Maddy and Jaxx walk in. She was shocked at how drawn and pale Jaxx looked. Normally cocky and tough, he looked like he had been through a war. *He has,* she reminded herself. *More than once.*

Maddy and Hope embraced, Hope hanging on just long enough to be sure she was in control of her tears, then she broke away and headed back to Bridger, who was sitting with Ryker.

"Where's Tank?" Jaxx asked, looking around the waiting room, assessing.

"He said he needed some space," Jennifer replied as she came up behind them, just returning from the ladies' room. She gave him a swift hug, and he returned it carefully. He was surprised. Jennifer never initiated contact. In a few short hours, everyone and everything had changed.

Jaxx moved down the hall, his eyes darting, searching. He didn't see Tank. He knew Tank was going to need help. He gave a low whistle and Betty was by his side in an instant. A quick glance told Maddy that, for the moment, Jaxx was fine. Reluctantly, she let him go. She wanted to be there by his side, but he had Betty. She would do her job.

Jaxx found him in the chapel. He and Betty paused in the doorway and watched for a minute. Betty whined softly knowing she was needed, wanting to help the broken soul who was in the pew. Tank had slid to his knees, his arms over the back of the pew in front of him clasped tightly together, wet with tears. His head rested on those hands, the picture of abject despair. His shoulders shook as he sobbed, a broken man.

Jaxx knew better than to go to him. A man needed this time alone. He put his hand on Betty's head and faded back into the hall, finding a bench. He pulled out his phone and texted Maddy.

`I'm fine. I found Tank. I'm going to stay`

```
here for a bit. Let me know if you need me or
if there's news.
```

Maddy immediately texted him back.

```
Thanks. I'll let you know. If you guys need
food or drink, I have it for you.
```

He smiled to himself. That was his Maddy. Feeding people helped her cope, taking care of people. He loved that woman.

Jaxx waited.

Tank prayed.

Betty watched them both.

16

An hour later, Betty sensed a shift. She picked her head up off her paws, her eyes watching the man in the chapel. She rose to her feet and looked at her master. Jaxx nodded.

Betty's large paws made their way silently down the chapel aisle. When she reached the row where Tank was sitting, she moved carefully toward him, her eyes never leaving his face. By now Tank's head was off his hands and he was staring at the stained-glass window in front of him. It was of Jesus on his knees, his face lifted to Heaven with a look of calm radiance and peace. He didn't feel any peace.

Betty laid her chin on his thigh. It didn't startle him. He was numb. He looked down at the dog, then looked around for Jaxx. He didn't see him, but he knew the man had to be close by. Betty leaned her chest into Tank and wiggled her chin against his leg, commanding that he pet her. Tank sighed and dropped his hand to her head, stroking the warm hair and soft ears. She leaned harder. Tank moved his other hand to her face until he had both hands on each side of her head. She moved her paws to his lap, transferring her weight onto her back legs. She looked Tank in the eyes. His hands moved until they surrounded her neck and he pulled the giant dog toward him, burying his face in her neck. He began to sob, emptying his soul. He had thought he was empty, but the dog knew better.

*J*axx watched his dog work. It wasn't often he got to see the miracle that was Betty. When she was there for him, he wasn't always cognizant of her talents. He just benefitted from them. Now he got to see what she did for him and what she could do for others. He was a lucky man.

A few minutes later, Tank sat up and Betty dropped to her feet. At the same time Jaxx's cell phone chirped.

```
A nurse just came out and said a doctor would
talk to us in a few minutes. Can Tank come?
```

Betty looked back to her master. She turned and licked Tank's hand then looked to Jaxx. Tank turned around.

"Hey," he said, not caring that his face was raw from the shed tears.

"Hey," Jaxx said, letting him know that it was alright. "The doctor is going to give a briefing in a minute. Can you come?"

Tank was out of the pew in a shot, almost falling over Betty in the process. She scrambled out of his way, not offended in the least. She followed, giving him space. When Tank reached Jaxx, he offered his hand. Jaxx shook it and pulled him into an embrace.

"Hang in there, buddy. I've seen worse."

"Yeah, but did they live?"

"Some did, some didn't," he admitted, "but let's have faith."

Betty fell in beside Jaxx and they made their way back to the waiting room and the gathering of friends who were determined to be there for the duration.

They arrived just as a doctor approached Ryker.

"You're her brother, correct?" the doctor asked, addressing the shell-shocked man. Jennifer reached and took his hand, a united front.

"Yes," he said, his voice sounding strained.

"Would you like to talk privately?" The doctor glanced around at the number of people gathered.

"No, please speak freely in front of them. They're all family." Ryker's eyes found Tank's. "Come over here, Tank, so you can hear."

Tank joined Ryker on the other side, Betty leaning against his legs. The doctor noticed and took a deep breath. This was going to be hard.

"Your sister has suffered numerous injuries. She's in critical condition, and to be honest, her prognosis isn't good. If, and I mean if she makes it through the night, her chances will improve slightly. Only slightly. She has a lot of surgeries ahead of her and any one of them could end badly. We have a tentative treatment plan, but we may have to make some sacrifices in order to save her life."

"Sacrifices?" Ryker echoed.

"Correct. Right now, a vascular surgeon is working to correct the damage to her left leg. He is at a critical point. He will be making the decision soon whether to continue attempting the repair or just take the leg. An amputation would be quicker, and quite frankly, probably a better choice with the end goal of keeping her alive."

Jennifer paled, but took a deep breath. She was determined to be strong for Ryker. The rest of them digested what the doctor was saying. Jaxx stood stoic. Been there. Done that. Chomps had come through fine though. His leg was hanging in tatters after the IED had done its work. It was amazing how quickly Chomps had adapted to the prosthetic. He'd gotten a dog, too. Ruger had helped with that transition. Amputation was a good plan.

"Her leg? No..." Ryker's eyes misted. "Can't you save it?"

The doctor looked frustrated. He had more to tell, and he had to get back, and the guy had just missed the point. Amputation might mean life.

Jaxx moved closer to Ryker.

"Man, it's not that bad. One of my men lost a leg. Sure, it was tough for a while, but he managed. Maeve is tough. She will manage. Let the doctors do what's best."

"Exactly," said the doctor, relieved that there was a voice of reason. "Once we get her stabilized from that, we will have to begin working on her face. To put it in layman terms, the bones in her face have been broken and have collapsed, smashed inward. She can't breathe without being intubated." He read the confused looks. "She has breathing tubes, she's on a ventilator, and she will eventually have feeding tubes. Essentially her face doesn't work. There will be several surgeries to repair her face the best we can."

No one had seen Jeff walk in and approach the group. He hung on the perimeter, listening to the prognosis. His beautiful Maeve, destroyed. He hadn't seen her. Didn't understand the extent of the damage, but her face needed to be repaired? He felt sick.

"What about the metal piece, I think it was the turn signal lever. It was stuck in her shoulder?'" Ryker asked, fixating on the thing he saw, the horror of the foreign object sticking out of his sister's body."

"Actually, that wasn't really a big deal." He smiled with the encouraging news. No one else shared his sentiments. "Okay then, I need to get back. I'll let you know what develops. Thank you." With that he shook Ryker's hand and turned, leaving the already bewildered group to digest the new information.

"Hello, Jeff," Tank said, as he reached out a hand to shake his rival's. Jeff reciprocated, his mind reeling.

"I would have come earlier," he stammered. "I just heard. My God." His voice trailed off, not sure what to say.

"You're here now," Hope said kindly.

They stood around awkwardly, wanting to talk, to hash over what the doctor said, but felt the strain of an interloper in their group. Betty whined, unsure of where to put her attention. Everyone needed her. The new guy not as much. She turned her attention from him and checked Tank and Jaxx. Mind made up, she sat next to Tank and licked his hand.

"Okay," Maddy said, determined to bring them all together. "It's going to be a long haul. It's time to eat." She moved to empty a nearby low table of its magazines. Hope stepped over to help her. Jennifer took one look at the table and shook her head. She walked over to the nurses' station and came back with some sterilizing wipes.

"Good call," said Hope, as she waited for Jennifer to scrub the table.

"Maeve taught me well," she said, then burst into tears. Ryker was at her side in two steps, pulling her into him, holding onto her for dear life. Embarrassed, Jeff moved away from the group. He didn't belong there with them, but he did belong with Maeve. He was torn.

"Jeff, you're welcome to stay with us," said Maddy. "I imagine you feel out of place. We've all been friends for a very long time. Most of us grew up with Maeve, but that doesn't mean you love her any less. It's okay. You're welcome here."

"Jeff, stay with us." This time it was Tank. "We all love her and now is not the time to say who loves her more."

Maddy walked up to Jeff and offered him a sandwich. He took it gratefully and smiled.

"Thanks." He stood awkwardly, waiting for Maddy to hand one to everyone. Jennifer took Ryker's after he stood and stared at it for a minute. When Maddy reached Tank, he waved it away.

"I appreciate it Maddy, but no thanks."

"I understand how you feel, but what would Maeve say?"

"She would chew my ass and tell me to eat."

"So, respect Maeve and eat the damn sandwich." She gave him a wan smile and squeezed his arm.

"Good point." He grinned at her, despite his pain, then suddenly pulled her into his arms. "Thanks, Maddy. I love you. Thanks for reminding me what Maeve would have wanted."

"You bet. We're in this together. We'll take care of each other so we can take care of Maeve. She's going to need us when she wakes up.

"That's right," said Jaxx. "We need to talk." He gestured toward the chairs and low table and they all gathered around, finding seats. Maddy offered drinks from the cooler making sure everyone was cared for.

"What's on your mind, Jaxx?" asked Bridger, knowing Tank and Ryker were still dealing with the demon leg.

"Maeve owns and runs a business. It's her livelihood. It's her life."

"You're right, Jaxx. It took a hell of a lot of convincing to get Maeve to leave it for the few days we spent at Nag's Head together," said Jeff. He said it without thinking of the ramifications. There was an awkward silence as Tank leveled a steely gaze at him.

"So, we need to chip in and keep it going," Jennifer said. "Bridger, can I divide my time between the marina and the diner? I'll make sure the marina books are all taken care of and not neglected."

"Of course, honey."

"I could probably try my hand at waitressing," Hope said. I've got time between my summer school hours and tutoring.

"Waitressing and running the business end are two different things," Jeff said, thinking about all the things Maeve was worried about before they left: the ordering, stock rotation, schedules...

"No kidding," Ryker replied, somewhat sarcastically and was immediately contrite. "I'm sorry."

"No worries," Jeff said, feeling guilty for bursting their bubbles. They all noticed he didn't volunteer a shift.

"I've got it."

All eyes turned to Tank. His demeanor had changed. He stood up, looking down on them.

"What do you mean?" Ryker asked.

"I mean I've got it. I'll take care of it. I'll make sure Maeve has something to come back to. I've got it." He drained his can of soda and pulled out his cell phone.

They all watched in silence.

"Hey, Pete, it's Tank...yeah, she's banged up pretty good. Can you handle closing up the diner?" He looked down at his watch. "Shit, I didn't know it was that late. Sorry. Okay, thanks for taking care of it. Are you able to handle everything in the morning? The open and the prep work? I'll call Susie and ask her to come in an hour earlier if possible. Okay, thanks, and I'll keep you updated."

He ended that call and put another one in to Susie. A few seconds later, he pocketed his phone and walked back down the hall toward the chapel. This time he wasn't helpless. Now he had a job to do.

*T*ank found the chapel empty. *Good,* he thought. *I've got some thinking to do.* He bowed his head, but he wasn't praying, not in the traditional sense. He just expected guidance as he sat there, making plans, figuring out schedules. He didn't want to do it in front of his friends. *Scratch that. I don't want to do it in front of Jeff.* It wasn't fair, and he knew it. Jeff was hurting too, and at a loss. Everyone was helpless right now, but he was going to fight. He was going to fight to keep Maeve's life going as she fought to keep herself going.

His lists finished, he said a quick prayer for good measure then stepped into the hallway. It was empty. He pulled out his phone again and made another phone call. This time to the one person he knew who could teach him the ropes.

Izzy.

When she answered, he talked and she listened. When he ended the call he knew what he was in for. He had a lot to learn, but he would have help. Izzy was as determined as he was to make sure Maeve had something to come back to.

He took a deep breath and worked his way back to the group. Betty stood up and came over to him, whining a little as she looked up into his eyes.

"I'm okay, girl. Thanks for being there." He crouched down and took the dog's soft ears into his hands and gave them a good scratching. Betty moaned in pleasure. There were perks to helping humans. This was one of them.

The group sat in silence and waited. They held hands and stared unseeing at magazines. The minutes ticked by excruciatingly slowly. Maddy cleared away all the debris from the food she brought and threw it away in a nearby trash receptacle, then she came back, and paced away again. She made a quick phone call to Mary to check on Belle. All was well there. Mary told her that the new girl, Lynn had tossed a giant t-shirt over Belle's head and then let Belle fingerprint to her heart's content. There were masterpieces awaiting Jaxx and Maddy when they finally came home.

When Maddy shared the story, everyone smiled…for a minute.

They waited.

The minutes slowly slid away into the night.

Suddenly, they heard the squeak of shoes on the floor. Tank was up like a shot.

The doctor.

He looked exhausted.

"At this point, we were able to save her leg, but that isn't any guarantee."

"What does that mean?" Ryker asked wearily.

"Any number of things can happen. Infection, for one. We just have to wait and see."

"What about her face?" Jeff asked.

Tank looked at Jeff. He didn't like the way Jeff asked the question. *Stop it,* he told himself. *It's the next logical question.*

"We won't do that surgery for a couple of days. I want her to stabilize some."

"You mean you are just going to leave her face that way?" Jeff asked incredulously.

"Yes, I am. She can breathe and get nourishment. She is in a medically induced coma right now to help her heal from her injuries and concussion, so she doesn't even know any different. This will also allow some of the swelling to go down, which will make the surgeries easier. For now, you should all go home. There is nothing for you to do here."

"Can I see her?" Ryker asked. "Can I just see my sister before I leave?" His voice broke with the last word.

"For just a second, but you need to be prepared. There are a lot of machines and tubes, and you can only stay for a second."

Ryker nodded miserably and followed the doctor down the hall. The others waited in a tight circle, wishing they could be there with him but knowing this was best for Maeve.

He came back a couple of minutes later a completely broken man.

*J*axx picked up the tote and took Maddy's hand. Betty fell in step next to them. They followed Hope, Bridger, Jennifer and Ryker out the door, Jennifer holding the truck keys in one hand, Ryker with the other.

Jeff had already left shortly after Ryker had come out of the room. He felt like an intruder. He didn't belong there. He didn't want to be there. He wasn't wanted there. He said his goodbyes and exchanged phone numbers. Promises were made to get in contact with him if there were any changes.

Just before Jaxx walked through the door to the outside, Betty stopped and turned looking back. Tank was still back in the waiting room. She whined, looking at her master.

"Hang on, Maddy," he said, setting down the cooler tote next to her. He and Betty walked back to Tank.

Tank watched them come. His face was an unreadable mask. Jaxx knew that drill.

"Hey, not following us?"

"No, I don't think so."

"You know there isn't anything you can do here tonight, right? You know that they won't let you in, right?"

"Yeah, I know."

"But you're still going to stay here, right?"

"That's right."

"Okay. Call me if you need anything. I'll see you in the morning."

"Take care of Ryker for me? Please, you and Maddy take care of Ryker?"

"We will. He's got Jennifer, and Bridger and Hope will be there for him, too. Maddy and I are here for you, too. Got that, Tank?"

"I do. Goodnight, Jaxx."

"Good night. Oh, and Tank, I noticed the shift change is coming up. You might use that information to your advantage." He lay a hand on his friend's shoulder, then turned and caught up with Maddy. The three of them left Tank there to hold down the fort.

Tank settled in a chair that gave him a direct line of view to Maeve's room. He watched the rhythm of the nurses, the movement in and out of Maeve's room, the grim faces, the casual joke between colleagues, the acceptance of life and death as a daily routine.

He wasn't here to accept.

The shift changed. He watched the nurses go over the charts. He watched the new shift go into Maeve's room. He figured out the leggy blonde was new. She would be easy. The salt and pepper, short older woman would be the challenge. As they left Maeve's room and moved down the hall, he stood and stretched. When they entered a room several doors down, he slipped in Maeve's door.

The lighting was soft. The machines beeped rhythmically. Maeve looked so small obscured by tubes and hoses, bandages and bedding. Her blonde hair still held remnants of the accident, dried blood matting the golden strands. *She would hate that*, he thought, his heart breaking for his Maeve.

He spotted a chair against the wall. He knew he would have a better chance of getting away with being here if he were as out of the way as possible, but he was determined to be by her side. He looked at the bed deciding just where he would be less of a bother. He moved the chair and settled himself in and reached between the metal frame of the bedside. Her hand lay on top of the bedcovers. It, too, was crusted with blood. An IV needle was inserted in the vein, taped in place. He wanted to hold her hand, but he didn't want to hurt her. Instead, he carefully slipped his hand under hers so it rested on top of his.

"Maeve, honey, I'm here for you. You don't do anything but rest and get better," he said softly. "I know it's probably gonna be impossible for you, but don't worry. If that brain of yours is working in there, trying to figure out how to take care of stuff while you're in here, don't worry. I've got this. I've got you Maeve. I will always have you."

He bowed his head as the tears ran down his face, splashing on his thighs.

"I'll always have you, Maeve," he whispered. "I was just lost for a bit. I let you down, and I'll never do it again. I will do what you want. I will honor what you want. If you love Jeff, I'll honor that, but I'll always have you. I promise."

He imagined her fingers twitched, but he knew better. She was in a coma. He was grateful for that. At least she didn't feel any pain.

17

*T*ank sensed movement. He opened his eyes, startling a little. He hadn't meant to fall asleep.

"Sshh." A hand pressed down on his shoulder. In the dim light he saw it was the older nurse. He prepared himself for a fight.

She shook her head and smiled.

"Sshh." She unfolded a blanket and tossed it over him, then handed him a bottle of water. "How's our patient doing?" she asked quietly glancing at his hand under hers.

"You tell me," he said, his voice gravelly.

"She's breathing...with the help of the vent. Her face is swollen, but that's to be expected. Her toes are pink. We are grateful for that. Your sister is holding her own." Tank didn't correct her.

She efficiently checked Maeve's vitals then glanced down again at his hand.

"Your arm is going to cramp up if you continue to hold your *sister's* hand like that." The emphasis wasn't lost on Tank. "It's good for a girl to have a lot of brothers. They'll be there to protect her. Now, you rest easy. The doctor will do his rounds about two hours from now. I'll be in just before that. You might consider finding yourself in the waiting room before he comes."

She winked at him and patted the blanket around him, fussing just a little. He smiled at her.

"Thank you," he whispered.

"You're welcome. Just keep doing what you're doing and pray. Love heals better than doctors." With that she turned and left the room. Tank took a swig of his water and watched the vent pumping air into his Maeve. It was steady. He would be steady. He had her, just like the vent did.

True to her word, Dottie, according to her nameplate, woke Tank a few hours later. She folded the blanket and stored it in a little closet. She also showed him a stash of water and snacks that had found their way there.

Tank stood, stretched, then impulsively hugged the nurse. She let him, patting his back.

"It looks worse this morning, honey, but that's to be expected. The swelling in her face is bad. In a couple of days, it will subside, and the doctors will be able to go in and start to do the repairs. Until then, these tubes will help to keep her alive. Look at them as her friends, like you. They are here to support her, but they aren't going to take over her life. Got it?"

"Yeah. I got it. Is she in pain?"

"No. Not now, but she will be. We will manage it for her."

"What about addiction?"

"Does she have a problem?" The nurses head snapped to attention and she regarded him shrewdly.

"No, ma'am. As far as I know, Maeve has never touched drugs. She drinks occasionally, but not heavy. It's just, we have a friend. She's an alcoholic. It reminds all of us the dangers..." His voice trailed off.

"Good. Then you and Maeve are aware. We will cross the pain bridge when we get there. One step at a time. Got it?"

"Got it," he said, his eyes scanning Maeve's beautiful, wrecked face.

"Good, now git before I get in trouble."

Tank picked up his water bottle and scooted for the door. He checked the halls. Empty. He turned and winked at Dottie then walked to the waiting room.

It was early, but Jaxx was standing there with a cup of coffee waiting for him.

"How is she?"

"The same," Tank answered taking the coffee gratefully. "Thanks, buddy."

"No problem. Maddy packed you some breakfast. I don't know if you feel like eating but she told me to tell you if you don't eat, she will tattle to Maeve when she wakes up."

"Girls play dirty."

"Yes, my friend, they do."

They sat together, sipping their coffee in silence. A half hour later, Jennifer and Ryker walked into the waiting room.

"Hey," said Ryker. He looked better than he did last night. There were dark shadows under his eyes, but today he looked like the old Ryker, ready to tackle any problem that came his way.

"You spent the night, didn't you?" Jennifer asked Tank.

"Mmmm…" Tank said, not committing.

"Thank you," Ryker said. "Thank you for watching over my sister."

"Oh look, the rest of her brothers are here."

Ryker looked up, confused as Dottie approached the group.

"Let me guess, you're her brother, too?" she addressed Jaxx. He grinned at her.

"We are all brothers, sworn to never leave another behind," he replied.

"I'm her brother," Ryker said, still not quick on the uptake.

"I know," Dottie said kindly. "The nurse last night clued me in on the dynamics here. So, the doctor is in with her now. He's encouraged about her leg, but still cautious. There's still a risk she'll lose it. I'm not telling you anything you don't know, and I'm not speaking out of turn here. He asked me to come out and let you know that and that she is doing well otherwise. He wanted to come talk with you himself but was called down the hall for another issue. He also wanted me to tell you that you can visit her one at a time. Talk to her. Tell her you love her. We never really know what gets through to a patient. Telling her you love her can never hurt." She turned to get back to her other patients, tossing over her shoulder, "just let me know if you need anything."

They thanked her as Ryker turned to go down to see his sister. Jennifer squeezed his hand before he left.

"I love you," she told him. He gave her a quick kiss and walked into Maeve's room.

A minute later a phone started ringing in Jennifer's pocket.

"It's Ryker's work phone," she said as she pulled it out, looking at the number displayed.

"That's the tile guy on the clinic project," Jaxx said looking over Jennifer's shoulder. She handed him the phone, a pleading look on her face.

Jaxx smiled at her, his eyes calming her in an instant.

"Wynn construction, Jaxx here." He moved away from the group and stood looking out the window as he handled Ryker's business. The call snapped Tank into action.

"I have to go for a little bit. Is anyone staying here?" Tank asked.

"Ryker and I will be here," Jennifer assured him.

Tank waved at Jaxx as he headed out the door. Jaxx waved back and shrugged, turning his attention back to the problem with the tile on the third floor bathroom. As he listened to the man complain, he reminded himself why he liked working for Ryker and not owning a company himself. It was a pain in the ass. But he would welcome taking the burden from Ryker as long as he needed.

Problem solved, he came back to the group at the same time Ryker came out of Maeve's room. Ryker was pale, but not as shell shocked as yesterday. Today was a new day, and they were all ready to do whatever it took to help Maeve get better and hold the world together.

"Where's Tank?" Ryker asked, glancing around.

"He said he had some things to take care of and he left," Jennifer said. "He wanted to know if someone was going to be here, and I told him we were. Also, you got a phone call on your work phone. Jaxx took care of it."

"Yeah, problems with the tile on three," Jaxx said rolling his eyes.

"What's new?" said Ryker with a wry smile.

"Ryker, if you don't need me here, I'm going to head over to the clinic and make sure the crew has what they need. Then I'll swing over to the Darby house and check the cabinets. They should all be installed today. Is there anything else you need me to check on? After that I was going to go ahead and mount the doors on one back at the clinic."

"No, that's exactly what I would have done today. Thanks, Jaxx. I don't know what I would do without you. I'm assuming Tank isn't working for me today?"

"My guess is he went to the diner," said Maddy quietly.

"The diner?" Ryker echoed.

"Yeah. You were kinda out of it yesterday. He announced to everyone he was going to take care of it, remember? Jennifer was going to take a couple of waitress shifts, and Hope, too?"

"You're right, but Tank doesn't know the first thing about running a diner," Ryker said, shaking his head, a new problem for him to solve.

"He knows Maeve. He'll figure out the diner. Let him." Jennifer said, rubbing Ryker's back soothingly.

"Yeah, Ryker. You need to let him do that. Tank needs it." Jaxx knew all too well the driving need to fix the problems of his fallen comrades. When Gary died, he roofed Lacy's house and covered the cost of daycare for their baby so Lacy could get back on her feet. The other guys helped, too. They carried their brother, and his family. No one left behind. Ever.

Maddy watched her husband's hand tremble slightly. It had been a bad night. He had nightmares. She didn't think he remembered upon waking, but she saw first-hand the terror he felt. Betty had spent the night on their bed. Maddy reached for his hand and interlocked her fingers in his. United. They would stand together for each other and for their friends. Whatever it took.

"Hey, Tank, booth or bar?" Susie greeted him with a smile.

"Not sitting," he said, not unkindly as he glanced

around the diner trying to assess how the morning was going. He wasn't sure if it would be crowded with people curious about Maeve or light because people had heard. The crowd looked normal, with the regulars in their normal places.

"Hey, Tank," said Manny. "How's Maeve doing?" The diner quieted with the question. Tank had to think quickly. Maeve wouldn't want anyone knowing her business, but these people were family, and news around Grey's Harbor traveled fast.

"She's hanging in there. Might be a little bit before she's back on her feet here," Tank said, hoping he did the right thing.

"That's what we figured," Ronny said, a laborer who shared the booth with Manny.

"Tank, give Maeve my best when you see her." That was Gabriel Mason, over in the corner with his son. The other customers murmured their best wishes, knowing that Tank wasn't going to reveal more, but he would be true to his word and pass their sentiments along. It was obvious no one knew Maeve was still in a coma.

"Hey, Tank," Pete, turned from the grill to see who had entered his kitchen. "Maeve doin' okay? I can't believe she didn't call and give me the business telling me how to run my grill." He grinned as he flipped several strips of bacon and a sausage patty.

"She's still sleeping," Tank said, figuring it wasn't actually a lie.

"Good, she needs to rest. Tell her we've got this, no worries. The only thing, I'm not sure what to do about the day's receipts. She usually locks those in the safe. I don't have the combination. I couldn't make a cash drawer this morning, but all the customers chipped in and paid correct change, or credit. That helped."

"I'll stop by tonight and handle the day's receipts. I'll also make sure you have a cash drawer tomorrow," said Tank, trying to make a list in his head of everything he needed to do. He ripped a sheet from an order pad and pulled a pen from the cup near the register. As he jotted down notes, the door of the diner opened and Izzy walked in. She nodded her greetings to the customers who spoke to her then made her way back to the kitchen.

"Morning, Izzy," Pete greeted. "Whatcha doing on this side of my grill?" he asked warily.

"Makin' sure you're doin' everything right. You know how Maeve is."

"Damn, she still has her eyes on me," Pete said, pretending to be mad. He turned his attention back to the grill whistling happily as he did the job he loved.

Susie came into the kitchen and added two more checks to his grill rail. She tsked at the coffee pot, seeing it was empty, but there were three orders up.

"Go on, Susie. I've got the coffee," Izzy said calmly. She set up the coffee station, brewing both a pot of regular and decaf. Once they were going, she reached out and plucked at Tank's sleeve. "Come on back here." She led him to Maeve's office. The door was unlocked.

Once inside she sat down behind Maeve's desk and picked up the phone, dialing a number she knew by heart.

"Hey, Bob. Izzy. Yeah, I know this is Maeve's number. She's going to be out of the diner for a bit, so I'm helping handle the orders. What does she have set up for this week…? That'll work. Okay, thanks, Bob."

She hung up and looked at Tank and sighed. She crossed the office and gently closed the door.

"Okay, I'm hearing rumors, but I want it from you. What's the deal? How is she, really?"

Tank looked steadily at Izzy. He steeled himself. He had shed a lot of tears and wasn't in the mood to do it again.

Izzy waited.

"Iz, it's bad. Really bad. She may lose a leg."

Izzy didn't flinch. Tank was grateful.

"She's in a coma, I think they said it was medically induced."

Izzy waited. Tank swallowed hard.

"Her face is destroyed. She slammed her face against something, and it broke her and pushed the bones inward."

"Brain damage?" Izzy asked.

Tank looked startled. He hadn't considered that. *Oh, shit.*

Izzy looked with pity on the man. His heart was shattered. It showed.

"They never said anything about that," Tank said, feeling the sudden desperate need to go back to the hospital.

"That might be a good sign then," Izzy said, moving in to give Tank a hug, but hesitating, watching him struggle to not cry.

"They said they would have to wait until some of the swelling goes down to do any repairs to her face." He stopped and snorted, a laugh that bordered on hysteria. "Repairs...like she's a fucking automobile."

He broke.

Again.

Izzy took him in her arms and let him.

"Here," Izzy handed Tank a soda. "Okay, this is the work schedule. We can't work Pete and Susie to death, but I know for a fact that both of them need the cash, so I'm sure they would be willing to do extra. You said Jennifer will come in... She's a pro, so that'll work out fine. Hope can learn, if she has the time between her summer school classes. Luckily, Maeve doesn't have this diner open long hours, so Pete and Susie can cover most of it."

Tank nodded, taking notes in a little notebook they found in Maeve's desk. He had already written down Bob's number for the product order. Maeve used only one distributor for all her supplies, both food and non-food, so that made things easier. Tank also found a stack of deposit slips in the top right drawer. Izzy called the bank and shot the breeze with Paula for a bit, softening her up. Then she let Paula know that she or Tank would be handling the deposits for the diner for the foreseeable future. Paula had heard Maeve was in the hospital. She let Izzy know that she would make sure the deposits were in the accounts Maeve usually used, but that was all she would do. No information would be forthcoming. She did confirm that they should accompany the deposits with the slips they found. Izzy said she would be taking a picture of each deposit daily and Paula agreed that it was a good idea.

After another hour, Tank's notebook was full of information and he felt more ready to handle holding the diner together.

As they left the office, they found Pete cleaning the grill after the morning crowd.

"Pete, I'm leaving for a bit. I'll be back to help you close up, but you'll need to tell me what I need to do. You can't do your job and Maeve's, too. I'm here to handle that end. You just need to let me know how and when."

"There is one thing, Tank." Pete looked embarrassed and uncomfortable.

"What's that, Pete?" Tank asked, Izzy watching carefully.

"Um, today is usually payday." He squirmed, wiping his hands on his apron.

"How much does Maeve owe you and Susie?" Tank asked reaching for his wallet.

"No, No. You don't pay us," Pete said firmly. "And Susie and I talked, and we can hold off for a couple of days."

"How does she usually pay you?" Izzy asked, thinking she remembered Maeve used a payroll service.

"She gives us an envelope and the check is in it. Sometimes she gets it from her middle drawer." Pete said helpfully.

Tank walked back to the office and opened the top middle drawer. There was a narrow divider that ran along the left side. In the divider were a stack of envelopes. Three were stamped ready to go into the mail, paid bills by the look of it, and two other envelopes were there, one for Pete and one for Susie.

Thank you, Maeve, Tank thought. *You're always so organized. Remind me to kiss you for that,* he thought, forgetting they were no longer an item.

18

Tank walked into the hospital just as Maeve was being wheeled out of her room and down the hall.

"She's getting moved out of ICU this fast?" he asked Hope. Then he saw the look on Ryker's face. "What is it? What's wrong?"

He didn't wait for an answer but sprinted down the hall after Maeve. Dottie caught him just before he reached the gurney.

"You need to let her go. They need to get her into surgery," she said kindly but firmly.

"I need to see her first. I need to tell her I love her." He shrugged off the hand that held his upper arm.

"Maeve," he called out. The gurney stopped for the elevator. "Maeve." He crouched and kissed her broken face. "I love you baby. No matter what, I love you and we'll get through this. I will carry you, babe. Wherever and however long you need. I will carry you."

The elevator door opened and Maeve disappeared. Dottie took his arm and led him back to his friends.

"What happened," he asked.

"Essentially, there was a blowout," Dottie explained. "Her leg was so badly damaged. The surgeon did what he could, but there was so little intact to work with. It didn't hold. The only thing to do is take her leg and move forward. She can't heal if she is fighting that battle, and there are so many more ahead of her."

Ryker groaned, sinking into a chair, scrubbing his face with his hands. Jennifer stood beside him, helplessly, not knowing what to do for him.

"What the hell happened?" asked Jaxx as he came through the door. He knew it was bad. He had only stopped to let Ryker know that the tile situation was solved and they were ready to start on the fourth floor, but he decided to make an executive decision for that later.

"They have to take her leg," Tank said. "She'll be fine. She is strong. She will be fine." He was starting to babble.

"Guys," Jaxx said firmly. "Look at me." It was a command.

They obeyed.

"This sucks. I know it does, but you accept it and move on. Maeve is the same with one leg as she is with two. She'll need help and strength, but she will not need pity. You guys can help or hurt, so I suggest you mourn for her leg now, but get over it and get educated. Figure out what she's going to need and then help her move forward."

Tank set his jaw, knowing that Jaxx was right. Maeve was still Maeve despite her new disability. Maeve was still the woman he loved even if her face couldn't be repaired. She was still Maeve, and he loved her. End of story.

"What's going on?" They all turned to see Jeff walking toward them. Hope took his hand and led him to a chair. Tank moved to the drinking fountain and busied himself there.

"Maeve suffered a set-back," Hope said gently.

"Oh my God, is she…"

"No, no, she is still with us," Hope hurried to tell him. "I'm sorry I scared you. But she's in surgery now. They have to amputate her leg." Hope patted his arm, trying to give him what he needed, but she just didn't know him that well.

"No," he said standing. "No, that can't happen. Her face. Her leg. What's left of her? Oh, dear God." He paced trying hard to reconcile the news. The rest of them politely gave him his space. There were no words.

They waited.

Again, time moved slowly.

This time it didn't take as long.

After all, they were taking, not saving.

*he doctor came to them looking exhausted. They gathered around, Jeff hanging off to the side. Hope noticed and pulled him closer into their circle. He smiled at her gratefully. She kept her hand on his arm, giving him support. She couldn't imagine how he felt, how he was dealing with this. She needed her friends, this group. He didn't have that despite the fact that they tried.

"That went as well as can be expected. The amputation is above the knee, but there is enough leg to support a prosthetic device easily. Normally she would go to a rehab hospital tomorrow, but we'll keep her here so we can address her facial fractures."

"Thank you, doctor," Tank said after he realized Ryker was at a loss for words. "Does she seem strong?"

"Actually, yes. She came through the surgery well. I have another doctor coming in tomorrow to evaluate the breaks to her cheek and orbital bones. I'm hoping we can get some of the swelling down so those surgeries can follow quickly, and we can get this lady healing."

Ryker nodded his thanks, still at a loss for words. Tank shook the doctor's hand.

"Can she have visitors?" Tank asked, as if he hadn't spent the night next to her.

"For a few minutes, and you need to scrub and wear a mask. We don't want any risk of infection. If anyone is feeling unwell, then please don't go into the room. Let's give Maeve every chance she needs. Any other questions? No? Then goodnight."

They all murmured their thanks and huddled together, gathering their strength. Ryker walked away from them and into Maeve's room. He came out immediately, bewildered. Dottie appeared by his side.

"They haven't brought her down yet. Give them a bit and she'll be back in her room shortly." She turned Ryker and steered him back to Jennifer. Jaxx felt sorry for him. Every time Ryker got it together, something else came along and shook him to the core. He needed to get his mind on something else. Jaxx walked over to him and pulled him away, explaining the issue with the tile setters and how he resolved it. Ryker engaged and they discussed what should be done tomorrow.

Maeve was moved back into her room and each one took a turn to stand by her bed, touch her arm, and whisper words of encouragement. Prayers were said, tears shed.

Tank told Jeff to go in before him. Jeff paled slightly then refused. He told them he was worried he was coming down with a cold and didn't want to risk getting Maeve sick. He told them goodbye then left, his head down, his shoulders sagging.

Izzy had come in and witnessed Jeff excusing himself. Her eyes narrowed. She knew where this was going. She slipped her hand into the crook of Tank's elbow.

"How's she doing?" Izzy asked.

"They had to amputate her leg," Tank answered, each time, the word felt foreign in his mouth. Izzy sighed and leaned into Tank. He put both arms around her and pulled her against him. This was the first time Izzy had to deal with Maeve's reality. It hit her hard.

God, I need a drink. The thought slammed Izzy, shook her core. *Where did that come from?* She thought. *Because I'm tired of being strong for everyone,* she answered herself. *I just want to get rip roaring drunk and mourn.* She shook her head. *It's good to want,* she reminded herself, *now pull up your big girl panties and stop feeling sorry for yourself.*

Tank pulled away and looked down at Izzy. He didn't like what he saw.

"You good, honey?" He recognized the look. The craving. He had seen it on Bridger's face when he lost his sister. Bridger didn't end up an alcoholic. Izzy wasn't so lucky with her pain. Alcohol had gripped her and never let go. Izzy was recovered, but the struggle was real. Would be forever.

"Yeah, I'm good. So, we've got another fight in front of us, don't we?"

"We do, Izzy, and we're going to win this one."

"She's strong, Tank. She's not the type to wallow in self-pity. And she's not vain."

"I know." He hugged her tightly, both of them gaining strength from each other.

"Stay here with Maeve. I'll run by the diner and handle the day's receipts and the deposits. You're going to have to learn how to do this, but not tonight."

"I was going to help Pete with closing. I know there is a lot of cleaning work that Maeve did."

"I'll have that covered tonight, too. Don't worry, we've got this. Maeve will have a diner to come back to. Now I've got to go talk to Ryker." She looked over and watched Jennifer, her hand on Ryker's shoulder. "Jennifer is so good for him."

"She's a lot stronger now, isn't she?" Tank said, smiling at the change in the young woman. "She has been a rock through this."

"She's a survivor, too. She'll help pull everyone along." Izzy patted Tank on the arm and walked over to Ryker, pulling him into her arms.

19

*J*eff stepped up to the bar. Izzy looked up.

"What can I get you?" she asked him.

"Bourbon, neat," he said

"Usually you're at the hospital at this time. Why aren't you with Maeve tonight? Is she doing okay?" she asked looking at him sideways while she poured the drink.

"I was earlier. She's still unconscious," he said not knowing why he had to explain himself to her.

"You're gonna bail on her." It was a statement, not a question.

"Izzy, you don't understand." He didn't deny it.

"Oh, I do understand. I understand very well."

"No, you don't!"

"Yeah, I do! You don't want to have the burden of taking care of someone. You don't want to have to put your life on hold," she said, no sympathy whatsoever touching her eyes.

"Izzy I've been there. I've done that. I put my life on hold while I cared for someone."

Izzy looked at him trying to read the truth behind those eyes.

"Izzy, my mom was a single mom. She got cancer and became very, very ill. I was in high school. I took care of my mother. I didn't go to parties. I didn't go to football games. I didn't go to college. I stayed with my mother, and I nursed her, and I cleaned her, and I fed her, and I did everything that I needed to do, and she still died. Finally, I was able to pick up my life again and go to college. I was able to move on. Izzy, I can't do it again. I can't stop my life again." He hung his head, embarrassed but resigned.

"Maeve's life has stopped," said Izzy, not caring to be kind. "Do you think about that? She didn't ask for this either, and you were supposed to be there to support her. You told her you loved her."

"Izzy, you don't understand. You don't know what it's like to give up your life when you're young to take care of someone!"

Izzy stared him down.

"I do know," she said. "You're preaching to the choir. The difference between you and me is I didn't bail. The difference is I really loved the person who needed me. You obviously never did. I'm going to make one suggestion to you. I suggest you clear out of this town. I suggest you pack your bags and find a new job because once everyone here in Grey's Harbor realizes you left her, once they realize you walked out on Maeve and left her when she needed you the most, they will turn on you. You will never work in this town again. They will never forgive you." She said it coldly. Not even feeling the least bit guilty about it.

Jeff drained his drink and set it down.

"Thanks, Izzy. At least you're honest with me." He left a stack of bills on the bar and walked out.

It was late. Tank was tired, beginning to feel the strain of splitting his time between his job with Ryker, running the diner, and sleeping in a chair next to Maeve. He had not left her alone at night since the accident and he had no intention of doing it now, despite his exhaustion and his body screaming to stretch out on a bed.

As he neared Maeve's room, he heard a voice talking, a man's voice. His heart leapt. *Was she awake?* He peeked in the door only to see Jeff's back to him. The man's shoulders were slouched and his head was bowed. At first Tank thought he was praying, and Tank was touched. Despite the fact that he loved Maeve, he didn't begrudge the fact that this man loved her, too.

He didn't mean to listen, but a phrase caught his ear. Leaving town. *What the hell?* Now he listened unashamedly.

"I'm so sorry, Maeve. You don't deserve this, but I can't do this. I can't be there for you like you're going to need. I am transferring to a satellite office. I wish you were awake so I could tell you to your face."

"No, you don't," Tank roared, forgetting to be quiet in the hospital. "No, you don't because you couldn't face her. You're a coward."

"Tank, you don't understand," Jeff stammered, jumping up and turning to face him.

"Yeah, I do. I totally get it. Maeve is no longer your show piece. She can't further your career. It'll take actual commitment to continue this relationship. Now get the hell out of this room and never come back you fucking coward." Tank moved to throw Jeff out, but the man scurried past him, his head down.

Tank ignored him. Jeff wasn't worth his time. He sat down in the chair next to Maeve and took her hand. The swelling in her face had gone down considerably. The doctors had told him earlier they were planning on operating in the morning to lift the bones back into place and pin them where they belonged. He didn't care what she would look like, he just wanted her to be able to breathe on her own, and he wanted her to wake up.

"Maeve, I'm sorry. I hope you can hear me, but I hope you didn't hear him. I love you Maeve, and I've got you. I will carry you wherever and whenever you need. I promise you that."

He settled in and told her about the diner, how he had made a big batch of her sausage gravy for the breakfast crowd. They were kind, but they said it didn't have the peppery kick that hers had. He told her that they all wished her well and hoped she could come back soon. They missed her cooking, but they promised they would keep coming even though she wasn't there.

He told her about the homeowner that gave Ryker a hard time

because the kitchen counter wasn't the right color. Ryker couldn't convince the woman that it was the same one she picked out. The *discussion* went on for half an hour until her husband came home and convinced her it was right. Then the husband told Ryker on the side that she was colorblind.

He talked into the night, until weariness took over. He woke when the nurses came in to check on Maeve, and when one of them covered him with his blanket. They had all settled into a rhythm with one goal in mind, caring for Maeve.

Tank was awakened early with the activity in the room. A doctor he had never met introduced himself and explained that they were going to go ahead with the facial surgery today. Maeve was currently being prepped and he would be lifting the bones. The doctor examined her carefully again consulting the most recent X-rays and the condition of her swelling.

"How long does this surgery take?" Tank asked, realizing he had some phone calls to make.

"I won't know for sure until I get in there, but I think it will be pretty straight forward. I am thinking I can do it all with one surgery." He patted Tank's arm. "I don't mean to be arrogant, but I am pretty good at what I do. She will be beautiful again. There's nothing I can do about that large gash and those stitches across her cheekbone. Maybe later she'll want to address that but let me work my magic. I'll take care of her. I promise."

Tank was touched. The doctors he was used to dealing with had been abrupt. They weren't mean or rude, just incredibly busy and they didn't waste words. This guy seemed like he wanted to hang around and shoot the breeze.

"Doctor, when do you think she'll wake up?"

"Honestly, that'll depend on her. We'll stop the drugs that are keeping her in the coma after the surgery is complete. Then, the waking up will be on her.

"Will she feel pain?"

"We'll control that with medications. We'll make her as comfortable as possible. I think her biggest issues will be accepting what has happened to her. She'll need a lot of fight to get herself back to functioning comfortably again. Does she have fight in her?"

"Ah, yeah. Maeve has fight in her, and I'll be here pushing her along," Tank said, his eyes misting,

"Then I don't know how she can fail." The doctor smiled and patted his arm. "Stay with her and keep talking to her for a little longer. They'll come to get her shortly."

"Thank you, doctor, and please," Tank looked at the man, holding his eyes "take care of her."

"Oh, I will," he said, eyeing the muscles in the tight black t-shirt Tank wore. "You scare me." The doctor smiled and walked out the door whistling tunelessly.

20

*H*ours had passed. It was night. The doctors had removed the ventilator, Maeve was breathing on her own and it should just be a matter of time before she woke up. The doctor figured it would be sometime the next morning or early afternoon. Tank had convinced everyone to go home and he alone was in Maeve's room. He had been holding her hand, talking to her, reminding her of the stories of their youth, bonfires at the haunted lighthouse, Frangelico-laced cocoa, all the transgressions of youth they shared. Her hand lay loosely over the top of his, as it had every night since the accident, ever mindful of the IV needle in the vein.

"Remember our first time, Maevey? It was night. You said I couldn't scare you with ghost stories. I bet you, but we couldn't agree on a wager. There was no moon, and the tide was low. The lighthouse was waiting for us, like it always was, ready to deliver its secrets.

"You brought a blanket. I brought some wine. It was cheap. I started to tell the old story of Madeline Aubuchon. You laughed, knowing the story by heart, you figured I would lose the bet. The night was completely still. Remember, Maeve? There wasn't any wind. Nothing to make the lighthouse moan as the breeze blew past it.

"Then, in the stillness, you heard the cry. It was a woman's cry, mournful and bleak. Do you remember what you did next, Maeve? You jumped into my arms. You were terrified. We could always explain away the ghost with the wind. Not this time."

He smiled at the memory, that night, Maeve's soft skin, her lips yielding to his. He lay her back on the blanket to sooth her and calm her, but she ended up trembling with anticipation. She looked into his eyes, and in the dark shadows of the lighthouse, they made love for the first time.

"Remember that night Maeve? I fell in love with you then and never stopped."

"It was the cheap wine and it tasted like shit."

"I was broke," he said. Then he realized what had happened. Maeve's hand squeezed his. He leaned over and looked into her beautiful green eyes.

"Hey," she said.

"Hey." He stood up and kissed her forehead gently. Her face was bruised and swollen again, but the sunken appearance was gone. The doctor said she was lucky that he didn't have to wire her jaw. *Small victories*, thought Tank.

"So, I kinda screwed things up, huh?" she asked, trying to shift in bed, her voice quiet and gravelly.

"Lay still, sweetie." He stroked her hair, "and yeah, you did it pretty good." He pressed the button that was attached to her bed to summon the nurse. "How do you feel?"

"I feel strange," she said. "Like things aren't working right."

With that the nurse came through the door, walking briskly to the side of the bed.

"Welcome back, Maeve," she said smiling. "I'm Dottie. Your boyfriend here and I have been spending the nights together, but I guess now that you're awake, I'm going to have to give up on that gorgeous hunk of man." Her practiced eyes looked over her patient and she checked her vitals. "Everything looks good, kiddo. What's your pain level?"

"My face is kinda throbbing." Maeve reached up to feel it, but Tank caught her hands.

"Leave her be," the nurse said kindly, "she won't hurt anything. Honey, your facial bones were fractured in the accident and you had a large laceration across your cheek. You have a bunch of stitches to close the cut and you had surgery this morning to take care of those broken bones."

"How bad do I look?" asked Maeve, trying to take in what the nurse was saying.

"Well, right now you won't win a beauty contest, but in a couple of weeks you'll be fighting off the gentlemen. Anything else hurting?" The nurse asked as she straightened the covers and fussed, giving Maeve time to assess herself.

Tank held his breath. Would she figure out her leg was gone. He felt physical pain thinking about how devastated she would be when she found out. How would he handle it? *Who am I kidding*, he thought, *I would be an asshole.*

"My shoulder is sore and my left leg hurts." She reached down to rub it. Tank moved closer to the bed. "What the hell?" Maeve croaked, her voice trying to find its strength. "What the hell?" She repeated, hysteria rising in her voice.

"Maeve, honey," Tank took over as the nurse nodded to him. "Your left leg was damaged really badly in the accident. The doctors tried to save it." He stopped, helplessly, unable to go on.

The nurse lowered the guardrail on the bed and finished what Tank was trying to say.

"The doctors had to amputate your leg. It's already healing nicely, and eventually you will be fitted for a prosthetic." She said it like it was the most normal thing in the world. She said it like everything was going to be just fine. Maeve, however, didn't see it that way.

She stared in horror, first at the nurse and then at Tank.

"Tank, please tell me she lying? Please, Tank." His heart shattered at the pleading in her voice. "Please tell me I'm whole."

He sank to the edge of the bed and carefully gathered her in his arms without lifting her. He leaned over her and breathed in her ear, murmuring to her.

"Maeve, losing a leg doesn't not mean you're not whole. Maeve, honey, you're alive. You're going to live. We were so afraid we were going to lose you. The doctors didn't think you were going to make it, but you did. I told them you were strong. I told them you were a fighter. So now, you need to fight."

He felt her stiffen. Pull away.

"They should have just let me die." She closed her eyes and locked herself away. Tank felt her do it. He let her.

The nurse beckoned him to the door and pulled him into a hug.

"She needs time. Don't take it to heart. Most patients say things like that when they find out that they've lost something. It's normal, I promise. Just stay with her and let her process her new reality. I gave her a little more pain medication in her IV, so I expect she will sleep. Sleep is what she needs now."

"She's been sleeping for days."

"Medically induced coma is not the same as sleep. Let her rest. Let her come to grips, and I am just a buzzer away. You get some sleep, too." She patted his arm and left the room, leaving him to pick up the pieces of his devastated Maeve.

21

"*W*hy are you here?"

"Because we're going for a ride."

"I'm in a hospital and missing a leg. I'm not going anywhere."

"As a matter of fact, you are." Tank tossed her a t-shirt and a flannel.

"What's that for?"

"It's about time you got dressed."

"This is fine." She gestured to her hospital gown.

"No, it's not." He held up a pair of jeans and some lacy underwear.

"You were in my house, going through my stuff?"

"No, Ryker and Jennifer were in your house. Jennifer picked out this stuff, and she packed a small bag for you with other stuff. So, you have plenty of stuff."

"I don't need plenty of stuff," she retorted. Then she smiled. She couldn't help herself. And Tank's world lit up. She was going to be okay. He just knew it.

"So, do I need to help you get dressed?"

"No," she said defiantly. She looked at him looking at her.

"What?" he asked, wondering what he forgot.

"Are you just going to stand there and watch me?"

"Sounds like a good plan to me." He grinned and wagged his eyebrows. She grinned then grimaced. "What's wrong, honey?" He was holding her hand instantly.

"It hurts when I smile." She pointed to the stitches. "Just a little, though."

"How about the rest, honey?" he asked immediately sobered.

"I'm not talking about that," she said. "Close your eyes."

"What?"

"I'm going to get changed, close your eyes." She clutched the t-shirt and flannel to her chest. Fear showed in her eyes, but she was determined to conquer it.

Tank closed his eyes, but he didn't want to. It's not that he wanted to see her body, he just wanted to be there if she needed help, to see it, to carry her.

He could hear her moving, swearing, struggling. He opened his eyes just a crack. She was stuck, a flannel sleeve not moving up the arm, twisted.

"Need help, Maeve?" he asked, pretending he didn't see.

"You looked," she accused.

"I did." He would never lie to her. He helped her with the shirt, pulling it carefully so he wouldn't hurt her.

She looked down at the panties and the jeans. She didn't want to do this part. She wasn't ready. She had refused to look at her leg, *her stump*, she reminded herself. The nurses had talked to her about caring for her wound, cleaning it. They showed it to her, encouraged her to look at it, to understand it. She wasn't ready.

But now, she had to dress. With Tank there. Which meant Tank would see it. *It, the abomination.*

"Maeve," he whispered, lifting her chin, seeing the hurt in her beautiful eyes. "It's okay. We've got this. I've got this. One step at a time."

She laughed sarcastically, tears springing to her eyes.

"Step?"

"Yes, Maeve, step. However we need to do it, and until you're ready, I will carry you."

Gently, he pulled back the sheets. He kept his eyes on hers as he slid her panties over her ankle and then over what was left of her left leg. She held his eyes with hers. He slid the jeans up being very careful of the tender healing end of her limb.

She helped by lifting her hips but slid sideways. Tank caught her hips and pulled the jeans in place. He pulled the wheelchair into place and locked the brake just like Dottie showed him.

"Ready?"

She tried a brave smile.

Tank leaned over and lifted her into his arms. She had lost weight. He remembered her so well. He had carried her before. It had been too long.

He held her for a minute, savoring her closeness, then he lowered her gently into the chair. Her fingers plucked at the loose empty leg of her jeans. He moved it into a more natural position.

"Where are we going?" she asked, curious now. It felt good to be out of bed. Suddenly she realized she wanted to be outside.

"We're going to the park across the street. I got permission to spring you for just a little bit. Then I'm taking you to your next appointment."

"Appointment?"

"Yeah, later, let's go to the park." He started down the hall happy that things were looking up. Maeve was pale and drawn, but she was no longer angry or feeling sorry for herself. He knew that it wouldn't last. He was warned. He knew that the next appointment, her first meeting with her physical therapist, was probably going to set her back. He was ready. He would be there for her, ready to push her, even bully her if necessary. He was going to get his Maeve back.

As he pushed her along the hall she asked questions about the diner. She hadn't been given her cell phone yet, her personal items had been taken home by Ryker. He wanted her to rest and not worry about business so he kept conveniently forgetting her phone, but Tank knew that she needed to get back to work, even here in the hospital. He handed her his cell.

"Why don't you call Pete?"

She looked up and smiled, radiant for a second, then unsure of herself.

"Just call." She pressed the number for the diner. Pete answered. The conversation was stilted at first, hesitant, but in a minute, Maeve was full on managing, telling Pete what to do, asking Tank to take a note, ticking off lists from her head. Tank knew Pete's head had to be swimming, and he never did take those notes for her. He wasn't one to carry paper and a pen in his pocket.

She ended the call and handed the phone back to Tank, a thoughtful look on her face.

"Thanks, Tank." She was lost in thought.

"What's wrong?"

"Nothing. Oh look, the sun is shining."

He pushed her through the automatic doors and down the side-walk. They waited for the walk signal then he moved quickly across the street, acutely aware of protecting her. He could tell she felt vulnerable.

"Under a tree or out in the sun?"

"Sun," she said firmly.

He parked the chair next to a bench then sat down beside her.

"Not like this," she said to him, looking at him expectantly.

"What do you need? What can I fix?'

"Can I sit on the bench? Next to you? Like a normal person?"

He didn't bother to tell her she was a normal person. He knew what she meant. Honestly, he would have felt the same way. He scooped her up in his arms and settled her on the bench, then sat next to her, his arm around her shoulder.

"Good?" he asked.

"Good." She leaned back and tilted her face to the sky soaking up the rays. He watched her face relax, a soft smile pulling at the corners of her mouth. "Tank," she said without looking at him, "I'm tired of being in the hospital."

Good, he though. *That's the opening I needed.*

"Okay, then let's work on getting you out. You understand you have to be able to take care of yourself to go home, right? The talk right now is of a rehab hospital."

"Someone mentioned that. I may have ignored them."

"What a surprise."

"I've been fighting them. I didn't want to sit in a chair. I didn't want them to show me how to pick myself up."

"I know, Maeve. It's okay. Are you ready now?"

"I want to go home."

"Then we have a lot to learn."

"We?"

"You aren't doing this alone, Maeve. I promise."

She was quiet for a minute, her eyes still closed, face tilted to the sun.

"I could hear things when I was in the coma."

He waited, silently, thinking of all the things he had talked about, not regretting any promises he made.

"I heard Jeff, or at least I think I did."

"I'm sorry, honey." He took her hand and pressed it between his own.

"It's okay. It wasn't right anyway. We weren't right. He wasn't right."

"I know. He tried."

"Yeah, too hard."

They both laughed.

"Tank, you don't owe me anything. You aren't obligated to be by my side."

"I love you, Maeve. There is nowhere else I'd rather be."

"I won't hold you to that love, or the things you said to me while I was out. You were desperate. You are afraid I was going to die."

"I was. All of the above. Most of all, I was afraid of life without you."

She opened her eyes and turned them on him, the startling green holding his.

"Tank, I broke up with you. I released you. I am not interested in a guilt-ridden man trapped with a broken woman."

"Goddamn it, Maeve. You are not broken. You are just wounded. I love you and I love your spirit. Your body is just a thing. God, don't you realize you're going to grow old? You're going to get wrinkles. Hell, I might even get fat and lose my muscle tone." He flexed, grinning. "But that's not what we love. We love our spirits. Jeff loved your beauty, and Maeve, you're still beautiful. Honey, I love your flaws and your scars, and your wrinkles, and your gray hair…" He reached and moved a strand aside.

"WHAT? On top of all of this, I'm going gray, too?" She reached up trying to snag the strand Tank had swept back.

"Here, look at it. It's beautiful, just like you." He leaned over and kissed her just below her scar, near the edge of her mouth. Her lips twitched. She turned to him, her eyes wide.

"I want to go home. I want to kiss you, but I really want to brush my teeth."

He laughed and planted a chaste kiss on her lips. He picked her up, holding her close, burying his nose in her hair. *I love you, Maeve, no matter what,* he thought.

"Then let's get you cleaned up, teeth brushed, and ready for your first therapy session."

"Therapy, already?"

"Actually, they tell me you're behind. Apparently, you refused."

"Maybe, a little. I'm ready now."

"Okay, but Maeve, it isn't going to be easy. It's going to be hard, but the only way to go home is to work your ass off."

"When have you not known me to work my ass off?" she asked, smiling that radiant smile that he loved so much.

22

"*W*hy is that wheelchair here?" Maeve demanded, impatiently.

"Hospital rules," Dottie said kindly, understanding the woman's frustration. Maeve had made amazing strides in the last couple days. Dottie had never had a patient change from giving up to being so determined to leave as Maeve. It was a good and welcome sign.

"Hey lady, are you ready to go home?" Tank came through the door anxious for this to be over. He wanted Maeve home and out of this place devoid of sunlight and fresh air.

"No."

Tank and Dottie looked at her, not believing her words.

"I want to go to the beach first. I want to sit by the ocean. Can we do that?

"Whatever you want, we can do."

"Only, if you make sure you use sunscreen on your face. It's very important, Maeve. I think I have some samples in the nursing station, if you hang on a minute." She hurried out and came back with several small tubes. "And Maeve, I don't mean to bring you down, but you are not ready to walk on the beach with your temporary prosthetic. The sand is too soft and uneven. I don't mean to be a buzzkill."

"Don't worry, Dottie," Maeve said, her eyes sparkling, "Tank'll carry me."

"You're damn right. Let's go."

Dottie hugged them both and wished them well, then Tank wheeled Maeve out of the hospital and into freedom.

She waited at the door with the security guard while Tank got his truck. She stood before he got out. His heart was in his throat. He wasn't next to her. *What if she falls?* He hurried to her side.

"I'm fine. I've got this." She walked stiffly to the truck, still not mastering the temporary leg, relying heavily on her arm crutches. The therapists assured her when her permanent one came it would be a lot better. There would be a learning curve, but she would be happier with it.

Tank opened the passenger door and looked at her dubiously. He knew he had to lift her in. She wasn't ready to make that climb or put that strain on her leg, but she had to ask for the help, as hard as it was for him not to jump in.

"I think I need help," she said, her lower lip between her teeth. She hated that she had to ask for help, but she wasn't stupid. The last thing she wanted was a setback.

In one swift move, Tank lifted her into the seat and made sure her legs were arranged comfortably. Then he closed and locked the door and got in the driver's side. He put the truck in gear and pulled away from the curb.

As he stopped at a stop light he glanced at Maeve. Her eyes were wide, her right hand gripping the door arm rest. She was breathing in short, shallow breaths, nearly hyperventilating.

"Maeve, honey?" She didn't answer.

He quickly pulled into a gas station and parked the car. She was still staring, almost in a trance, on the verge of panic.

"Maeve, are you okay?" He gathered her in his arms. Where had he seen this before? Someone else...

In a second she was recovered, shaking. She turned to him and smiled, trying to cover her fear.

"Sorry about that. I haven't been...since the accident...I just," she looked small and broken again, the fight gone. Once again, his heart broke. The road was going to be long.

❧

*M*aeve managed to walk down the wooden sidewalk to the sand under her own power. Her smile showed just how proud she was of her accomplishment. Every few minutes someone stopped to say hi and to give her a hug. She felt like she was being welcomed home. She tried not to feel self-conscious about the outward signs of her missing leg, her arm crutches obvious testament to her situation.

She was also surprised at just how tired it made her. Tank picked her up and carried her to one of the benches near the dunes. He sat her down carefully.

"Did you want to sit in the sand?" he asked, realizing he didn't have a blanket for her.

"No, this is perfect," she said as she watched the waves pull her pain away.

They sat in silence, holding hands, letting the ocean heal. When Tank glanced at Maeve her face was tranquil but determined. He thought the worst was over.

"Hey guys! Jaxx look, its Tank and Maeve!" Maddy ran to the bench, dropped on her knees and pulled Maeve into a giant hug. Jaxx came up behind her smiling.

"Hi, Maeve. You look well." Jaxx hugged her when Maddy finally let go. Betty pushed him aside and sat in front of Maeve. She sniffed her prosthetic once then lay her chin on Maeve's thigh, her liquid brown eyes searching Maeve's face. She whined softly and Maeve dropped her hand on Betty's head, petting her warm fur.

"Maeve, you okay here for a minute?" Tank asked, not willing to leave her if she said no.

"Of course," Maeve replied.

"I want to talk with Jaxx about some stuff."

"I'll sit with her," Maddy volunteered. She plopped herself down next to Maeve and began to fill her in on all the gossip in town.

Betty stayed with Maeve as Tank and Jaxx moved toward the water. Tank picked up a stone and threw it into the waves.

"What's on your mind?" Jaxx asked, knowing Tank well. Something was weighing heavily.

"Maeve had an…episode, I guess. In the truck."

"What happened?" Jaxx asked, but he had already figured it out, had been waiting for this.

Tank explained the look of panic and the stressed breathing. *All the classic signs of PTSD*, Jaxx thought. He sighed. *Another battle you guys have to fight.* He explained the syndrome to Tank, the symptoms and the ramifications.

"But it's not like she went to war, Jaxx."

"It doesn't matter. She suffered a traumatic event. The consequences of which were devastating."

Tank nodded, thinking about it. This was an invisible enemy he didn't know how to fight.

"I know what you're thinking, Tank, and you're right. You can't fight it, and Maeve can't fight it on her own. You need to recognize the signals, and you also need to realize that beautiful smile of hers is a mask she can hide behind. The smile makes you happy. She knows it. She can flash it to you and make you believe she no longer feels any pain or anxiety. But she does."

"Maeve doesn't lie," Tank said hotly, then immediately felt guilty

"It's not like she's lying, Tank. She is just trying to protect herself. Let me give you the name of my therapist. He specializes in PTSD. And if Maeve likes pets, a service animal is an amazing benefit."

They turned and watched Betty leaning on Maeve's good leg, Maeve's hands stroking the dog, gathering strength.

"In the meantime, anytime you need Betty to visit, just let me know. We will get her through this. She's doing remarkably well already."

"Thanks, buddy."

Jaxx clapped him on the back and they walked back to the bench. Maddy stood up and joined Jaxx.

"Belle is with Mary and Henry tonight and we were going to the Mizzen Mast for dinner. What do ya say? Join us," Maddy said, reaching for Jaxx hand.

"I don't know," said Maeve, patting her hair with on hand, her fingers fussing with the left pant leg with the other.

"Whatever you want Maeve. You can have Izzy food, or Harbor New York pizza, or anything else your heart desires."

"Come on, Maeve, a bar burger has to sound good after hospital food," Jaxx teased her. She had grown thin and he knew she needed to eat for strength.

"Up to you, Maeve, but we can leave the minute you say you're tired."

"I am kinda hungry. I'd like to see Izzy and thank her for helping you hold the diner together. I don't know what I would do without you guys, all of you," she said looking around at her friends, her eyes filled with tears.

Betty leaned against her good leg again and pushed her muzzle under Maeve's hand demanding to be pet.

"We're going to walk on over. My guess is you'll beat us." Jaxx called over his shoulder as they headed down the beach to the wooden sidewalk working their way to the river and the Mizzen Mast.

"It's okay, right?" Tank asked.

"Yes," Maeve said, but she wasn't completely convincing. She had only had her friends around her. They were used to her missing leg. The few friends she met on her walk were kind, but they were curious. She knew she would be the object of a lot of stares at Izzy's. She almost backed out. She didn't really want to go. *Do you want your life back or not?* She asked herself. She straightened her shoulders and made herself ready. She did that a lot lately. Made herself ready.

*I*zzy looked up from the bar, a slow smile spreading across her face. She wiped her hands on her butt and scooted around to meet Tank and Maeve.

"Welcome home, honey," Izzy said as she moved to Maeve, hugging her carefully so she didn't lose her balance.

"It's good to be here," Maeve whispered in Izzy's ear. Then unexpectedly, she burst into tears. She was mortified. She was in public. Izzy held her close, not letting the world see Maeve's pain.

"It's okay, honey. You've got this."

"I don't think I do. I can't breathe." Maeve gasped. Izzy kept her steady, looking over Maeve's shoulder and locking eyes with Jaxx across the bar. Tank moved in, bewildered, but Izzy shook her head; a warning.

Betty came out from under the table where she had been laying between Jaxx legs. She made a beeline for Maeve, weaving in and out of people until she was there, shoving her nose in between Maeve and Izzy, desperate to help the panicked woman.

"Maeve," Izzy said, as she steadied her. "Come and check my sloppy Joe's. Let me know if I have enough kick in there." Her commanding voice got Maeve moving, Betty following beside her. They made their way toward the kitchen, turning into Izzy's office before they got there.

She closed the door behind them, sealing them in the sanctuary that had been Izzy's escape over the years. She settled Maeve on the couch and crossed to the mini fridge next to her desk. She pulled out a bottle of water and turned around to find Betty sitting in front of Maeve, her head resting on her wounded thigh, Maeve's hands petting her rhythmically. The dog's liquid brown eyes held Maeve's, as she tried to get a grip on herself.

Izzy opened the water and handed it to Maeve. "Drink up, honey. It'll help."

"It's just water," Maeve whispered.

"Yeah, that's what you need now. Alcohol is not your friend."

"I know." She never stopped petting Betty, switching to one hand. "I don't know what happened."

"You had a moment. We all do."

"No, something happened, and it happened in the truck on the way home from the hospital. I panicked."

"Okay, so you panicked. Honey, you've been through hell. It would have broken a lesser woman.

"Izzy, I am broken," Maeve said softly. "I am broken in so many ways."

"No, you're not, honey. Things are different. You lost a leg. So, you're missing a part of you, but it's not the part of you that makes you who you are. Once you come to grips with that, it'll be easier."

"I'm trying, Izzy. I'm trying so hard." Betty whined and leaned into Maeve, demanding her hands keep petting her head.

"Maybe you shouldn't try so hard," Izzy suggested.

"What?"

"Maybe it's okay to rely on some people for a while. And maybe it's okay to lean on some friends and admit when you're having a hard time."

"I need to be strong. I need to get better."

"Yes, you do. But you need to let it happen on its own time. You need to let yourself heal, and that doesn't happen overnight. But most importantly Maeve, you have to let Tank know when you're having a bad time. He wants to be there for you and help you."

"I don't want to let him down. I don't want to disappoint him."

"You won't. Just be you. Who you are right now. What you're feeling right now, even if it means you're not strong right now."

ank was waiting outside the door when Izzy opened it. He eased back letting Izzy pass, his eyes never leaving Maeve. Betty walked up to him and shoved her snout in his hand, wet and cold.

"Hey," Maeve said, casting her eyes down for a minute.

"Hey," Tank said, suddenly realizing Maeve looked a little like Jennifer when she first came back to Grey's Harbor; broken, defeated, and hurt. For the umpteenth time that month his heart shredded.

He took her hand, squeezing it, trying to give her strength. Izzy watched them as they walked into the bar, Tank leading Maeve to the table in the back corner where Jaxx and Maddy waited. Betty wiggled under the table again and found her spot next to Jaxx, but rested her nose on the top of Maeve's foot

"What can I get everyone?" Izzy asked, like the last ten minutes never happened. Her practiced eye took in the fact that her guests had their drinks, but the menus were still there. No one would have ordered without Maeve anyhow.

Once they ordered, everyone started chatting, in an effort to keep Maeve comfortable. Eventually, she started to relax. Tank slipped his arm around her and gave her a squeeze, letting her know he was right there, ready at a moment's notice to leave.

In a few minutes Izzy came back followed by one of her waitresses. The trays were laden with food, burgers and onion rings for everyone. Izzy put a cup of soup in front of Maeve.

"Um, thanks Izzy, but I didn't order soup."

"I know you didn't, but I thought a cup of potato soup was in order."

"Thanks, Izzy. You know me well." She picked up the spoon and dipped into the creamy soup loaded with bacon, cheese and scallions. Izzy watched her expectantly.

"You changed it," Maeve accused, her brows furrowed trying to discern the taste.

"What?"

"You did. There is a different taste in here." She took another bite while the others watched with fascination. "I can't quite pinpoint it. It's an underlying flavor, subtle, very faint... there it is. Wait, it's hot sauce. You put hot sauce in here. Just a little bit. I put it in my macaroni and cheese, but not my potato soup. I think maybe I like it," she said hesitantly.

"No, you don't. You don't like it at all, and it doesn't work with the rest of the flavors. You're just being damn polite," Izzy teased her.

"Okay, you're right. It doesn't work. It doesn't set well with the thyme."

"You're right it doesn't. Hang on." Izzy swiped away the cup of soup and headed back into the kitchen.

"What's gotten into Izzy?" Maddy asked as she watched her walk back with another cup of soup.

"Here, try this one."

Maeve looked at her steadily, not really sure what the game was, but she dipped her spoon in the next bowl and took a bite. The soup was silky and savory, the thyme and a hint of rosemary making a background for the bacon, cheese and scallions. It was delicious. It was perfect. She smiled.

"Okay this is perfect, Izzy."

"Yep, and you knew it didn't you?"

"Of course,"

"Of course. The soup hasn't changed, and neither have you. Now eat your burger and onion rings before they get cold."

23

*T*ank opened the door to Maeve's house and watched her as she stepped in. It was quiet and peaceful, a floor lamp leaving a pool of light in the cozy living room.

"This'll be your first night alone," Tank said worried she would need help and no one would be there.

"I know. It's what I want," she told him with a brave smile. She had an aid with her every night since she left the hospital to help her if she needed to get up and to assist her getting ready for the day in the morning. Then the day aid came. Ryker had insisted, and Maeve hadn't fought him until today. Maeve was tired of her privacy being invaded. She had occupational therapy during the day, doctor's appointments, permanent prosthetics fittings, she hadn't had a moments peace. She hadn't been alone since the accident.

She was tired of people, the attention, the concern, the curiosity. She was just damn tired.

"I can stay, if you want." He knew she didn't want, but he didn't want to leave her either.

"I know you can. I need to do this, Tank. Please?"

He nodded. He understood. He knew Maeve better than she knew herself. He knew she was struggling. He also suspected she felt guilty about him. She had broken up with him, but she had been relying on him heavily. He knew she was confused. It hurt, but he was a patient man. He had made mistakes. Huge ones where Maeve was concerned. Now, he was determined to set it right, however she needed it to go.

"Okay, but I am just a phone call away. Promise me you'll call if you need me?" He held her chin gently, looking for the promise in her eyes. It was there.

"I promise. Goodnight, Tank. I've got it from here."

He kissed her chastely on the forehead. It was killing him to leave her, but he knew he had to. The time had come. He locked the door and pulled it closed, leaving Maeve standing alone for the first time.

S he locked the door and stood in her living room just looking around. She hugged herself. She was finally alone. In her house. There was no one here to ask her if she was okay. If she needed something. How she was feeling. How she was holding up. Just how the fuck she was.

"Well, I'm fucked. That's what I am."

She said it out loud, listening to the words echo off the walls in the empty house. *"I'm fucked. I can hardly shower by myself. If I have to pee in the middle of the night, I have to strap a fucking leg on because mine is gone. Removed. Discarded."*

A fat tear rolled down her face.

She was alone.

She walked to the bathroom and got herself ready for bed. Teeth brushed, face washed. She would shower in the morning. Just this morning she learned to use her 'shower leg.' That was a treat. She had a special leg for the shower. *Oh, happy day.*

She made sure she had everything she might need within reach of her bed, then she removed her prosthetic and pulled her stump shrinker on and crawled into bed.

Stump shrinker. The word was obscene. In fact, just the word stump was obscene. She hated it. She hated the look of her leg, the wound healing well, the doctors said. *Sure, it didn't happen to you.*

She lay down and there it was, like it was every night. She could feel her leg. It was still there. In fact, it hurt. There were stabbing pains that shot through her leg. The leg that wasn't there. The leg that fucking wasn't there.

She sighed.

She was alone.

She could cry.

She could scream.

She could throw a tantrum,

So, she did.

It started with tears. A few at first, then picking up speed. Then there were a lot of tears, complete with hiccups and shoulders shaking.

Then she got mad. She screamed. Then she screamed at God, following that up with a cursing out of the doctors, and Tank because he was so fucking nice, and then Jeff because he was a fucking coward. She remembered Tank calling him that. She had to agree.

Then she turned her anger on her prosthetic. The pathetic prosthetic. The temporary one because she was going to get a nice bright shiny one that fit and worked better. She looked at its shadow in the dark, her tears blurring her vision.

She hated it.

It was objectionable.

She didn't want it to be part of her.

"I fucking hate you," she screamed as she picked up the leg with both hands and attempted to throw it across the room.

It was heavy and awkward.

She didn't accomplish what she set out to do.

What she did accomplish was falling out of bed, hitting her head on the nightstand and crashing on her stump.

And that fucking hurt.

She gave up and lay there, crying silently against the soft, fuzzy sheepskin rug that she dearly loved. Where it looked like she was going to spend the night.

The sun rose over the ocean, casting the world in a soft, creamy yellow glow. The world woke and so did Maeve. Everything hurt. She wasn't sure if she had damaged her leg. She didn't want to look. The hand mirror was in the bathroom. They had showed her how to angle the mirror so she could check the skin on the end of her stump to see if she had any cracks or erosions. The stump shrinker didn't look like it had any blood seeping through, so she convinced herself that everything was probably alright.

She wanted to take a shower, that was the plan, but she didn't want her leg to swell from the heat. Still it would feel so good.

Damn it, she was a grown woman. She could shower if she wanted. She looked at the abandoned leg laying on the floor a few feet away from her. She would have to scoot herself to it. Maybe she could get herself in the chair so she could put the leg on.

It was a painstakingly slow process, but she eventually made it. She was exhausted. She lay there, trying to gather her strength. It was getting late and she wanted to get to the diner. Suddenly it dawned on her that she left her crutches by the bad. *Damn it.* She sighed. It was now or never.

She pulled on the chair with her hands, almost bringing it down on her. She shifted herself and moved her weight, balancing out her need for the chair and keeping the chair where it belonged.

She couldn't get her good leg underneath her.

She puzzled it out, frustration growing. She almost threw the leg again but thought better of it.

She took three deep breaths to calm herself then managed to lean her upper body over the chair seat while she pulled herself up onto her good leg.

Ha, she thought, *yoga does have a use*. She reminded herself to write a thank you note to the yoga instructor she took a couple of classes from a few years ago.

She hopped in a circle until she was backed up to the chair, then she plopped herself in the seat and rested. She was angry at the situation, but a little bit proud, too. Now she had to pee, and waiting was not an option. She attached her prosthetic and stood up. All was going well. A minute later she was in the bathroom and feeling successful.

Not bad for a tantrum hangover crash and burn. Now I just need to sit in a stupid chair, shower, dry my stump which still grosses me out, stick my leg on and get to the diner all in forty minutes.

She decided it was okay to cry a little bit more.

24

"*S*it, Maeve." Susie pointed to the table in the corner, a stern look on her face.

"I was going to," Maeve said as she sank into the chair. Her doctor told her she could hang out at work, do the books and the ordering, but she couldn't be on her feet, *foot* she reminded herself, all day. She had tried to stay out of the way, but the sausage gravy needed more pepper, and she needed to check the dates on the stock in the walk-in.

Despite her exhaustion, it was good to be back. The morning crew customers were happy to see her and welcomed her back like family. They all told her that the sausage and gravy was a whole lot better now she was back in the kitchen.

They all tried to not look at her misshapen pant leg, but she caught the curious glances. She hated it. For one wild moment she imagined taking down her pants and offering them to take a good look. It was everything she could do to not start laughing hysterically with the image. She got herself together with only a hiccup moment of near tears. Then she smiled her Maeve smile and dazzled the world with the fact that she'd gotten it together so quickly.

Jaxx walked in with Betty just as Susie brought Maeve a cup of tea. Susie glanced at Betty and asked Jaxx what he wanted to drink.

"Coffee, please. Black. Hey, Maeve," he moved toward her, Betty pushing ahead, happy to see her.

"Hey, Jaxx. Care to join me? Hey, Betty." Betty sat next to Maeve, who dropped her hand on the dog's head, petting her rhythmically. Suddenly that's all she wanted to do. Just pet Betty until her sadness disappeared.

Jaxx eased down into the chair across from Maeve and watched her carefully. He saw the signs; the drawn face, the circles under her eyes, the jerky movements and the desperate petting of Betty. Betty looked happy with the attention, and she knew she was doing her job.

"I'm not going to ask how you're doing. I know you don't want to hear those questions. Instead I'm going to tell you how you're doing. Are you ready?" He waited, training his intense eyes on Maeve's, soothing her with them. He knew how to manipulate people, for the bad and for the good. He wanted her to hear him and not get pissed. It would take some skill.

Susie came by and dropped off his coffee and the last of the maple iced cinnamon rolls from Anna's Bakery.

"Susie, I could kiss you, but then I'd need to fight your husband." Susie blushed, enjoying the attention then hurried away to take care of the cleanup from the morning rush.

Maeve waited until Susie moved away then turned her attention back to Jaxx. Her hand was still absently petting Betty's head.

"Go on." That was all she said. It was all he needed.

"Maeve, you're holding your world in tight, trying to stay in control. You're a ticking time bomb."

She started to protest, but he held up his hand. He crinkled the corners of his eyes with a smile, knowing it would work and she would sit back and listen.

Mission accomplished.

"You can go on like this if you want. I did. I came home battle scarred and carrying my brothers, the ones who made it and the ones who didn't. I denied that I was hurting. I was alive. I was only wounded on the outside. I was tough, and I was strong. I could carry them. I wouldn't burden them. I ignored my little bouts of temper, quick to anger. I looked past my hands when they trembled. I had a job to do and that was take care of my brothers' families and mine. And I did. I buried myself."

"Did it work?" Maeve asked. A simple question with so much meaning behind it.

"No."

Maeve waited, afraid of what was to come. Jaxx didn't talk about himself often. Maddy had shared that with her. She knew Maddy ached to help Jaxx with his demons but respected his privacy. She knew he would tell her when the time was right. Now he was opening up to her. She didn't like that. It meant he was worried about her. She didn't like that at all.

"When my wife and daughter were killed, I went crazy. I tried to find the man who did it. The monster. But I was helpless. I didn't protect them. Couldn't save them." His eyes turned dark with the memories. His hands started to tremble. Betty quietly got up and moved to her master, leaning her heavy body against his legs. "I'm okay, Betty." He gave her head a quick pat.

"I'm sorry," Maeve whispered, not wanting to imagine the pain and helplessness he felt. She knew she had nothing on him, but she also knew he wasn't telling her this to minimize her struggle. There was a different meaning here.

"Not your fault," he said. "My family was murdered by a man and the system, a system that doesn't step in and help people with mental illness." He paused to let that sink in. For both himself and for Maeve.

"The man was damaged?" Maeve asked.

"Aren't we all?" Jaxx replied.

They sat in silence for a minute soaking in the conversation. Letting it steep like the tea in front of Maeve.

"Maeve, if you don't get help, this will eat you alive. Someone told me the same thing, but I didn't listen. Too damn stubborn. I almost destroyed myself and another child before I came to grips with what I had to do."

"What happened?" Maeve asked as she sensed Betty getting even closer to Jaxx.

"I had an episode. I was driving. I have PTSD. You know that. Well, I didn't accept or acknowledge it at the time. I was driving down the road, but instead of the quiet neighborhood I was in, I was taken back to a dusty sand covered town, and the child on the side of the road was a suicide bomber. I needed to take him out so he wouldn't kill my guys. Except it was a little girl on a tricycle."

"Oh, my God, Jaxx." Maeve looked at him in horror. Betty snapped her head between the two of them trying to decide who needed her most. She stayed with her master.

"It's okay, Maeve. I didn't hit the girl. Somehow, maybe God had mercy on my soul, but I swerved my truck at the last minute. Then I knew I needed to get help. I found a therapist, and then I got Betty. It hasn't been easy, but Betty has helped, and talking to a professional has really made a difference." He slid a card across the table.

It lay there. Maeve staring at it.

"Pick it up," Jaxx commanded. She did. "Call the number when you're ready, or maybe before." He drained his coffee and stood up, kissing her on the forehead. "Maeve, we all love you. Some of us love you more than others, but sometimes love isn't enough. Sometimes, you need to take another step before you can love people back. Think about taking that step."

He turned to leave and Maeve stopped him. "Jaxx, when you first came to Grey's Harbor, Betty wasn't always with you. Sometimes she was wearing her vest, but most of the time not. Why is she with you all the time now?"

"'Cause I need her again, all the time. She knows it and I know it. Maddy knows it, too."

"Why?"

"Because shit happens, honey. Sometimes, shit just happens."

25

*I*t was early, and the senior dinner crew had just cleared the diner. There was a storm brewing, and the few diners that had been there hurried to finish so they could get home before the heavens opened up. Pete started cleaning the grill when he got a call on his phone. The ring surprised everyone. Pete never got a call on his cell.

Susie had one foot out the door. She had put in a long day and had plans with her husband. She was in a hurry. Pete waved her on as he answered. He had this.

Maeve watched from her office door, seeing Susie leave and reading the look on Pete's face. Something was wrong.

"What's up, Pete?" she called as she struggled to get up from her chair. She reached for her forearm crutches. She was hoping when she got her new prosthetic, she could lose the crutches.

"Penny may have broken her arm," he said, sighing.

"Oh no," Maeve hurried as fast as she could to get to Pete, but her crutch caught on the leg of her desk, almost pitching her sideways. *Damn it*, she thought, fury rising in her. *That's all I would need.* Swallowing her frustration, she slowed down a little, making her way carefully around her desk and out of her office.

"I swear, that child is going to be the death of me. Shouldn't she be playing with dolls or something?" The man looked so positively bewildered Maeve had to laugh.

"There is nothing wrong with being a tomboy, Pete. God knows I was one. How'd she do it?"

"Jumping off a porch roof," he said, remembering doing the same thing as a kid.

"Go, Pete," Maeve urged. "Is Laura taking her to the hospital?"

"Yeah, I need to meet them there, but I can't leave you with this mess."

"Why not?"

"Seriously, Maeve?" He didn't want to state the obvious, but he didn't want to leave her either.

"I've got this. You took care of most of it. I've been sitting on my ass all day. My therapist said I had to make sure I worked the muscles so they didn't atrophy. I've got it."

He stood hesitating. Uncertainty swirling around his brain. Still, his little girl needed him. She may be a tomboy, but she needed her daddy.

"Okay, but you want me to call someone?"

"NO. Go, Pete, before I get mad."

He hesitated another minute, then turned to go out the door.

"Don't make me regret this," he warned her. She waved him on.

She made her way over to the grill. She had cleaned it a million times before. It wasn't any different. She set to work, determined to handle everything by herself.

As Pete backed his car out of his parking spot next to the dumpster behind the diner, he made a quick phone call while glancing at the sky. He hoped the rain would hold off until he got to the hospital. His windshield wipers were a sometimes thing. He had been meaning to get them fixed. He listened to the ringing in his ear as he pulled onto the main road on his way to his daredevil princess.

"Hello?"

"Hey, Tank. It's Pete, from over at the diner."

"Maeve?"

"No, no. She's fine. It's just, she'll kill me if she knew I called you." He went on to fill Tank in on the situation.

"I was just going to go over there to see if Maeve was in the mood for some Harbor New York. No worries. I've got this. Tell Penny to take it easy next time."

Twenty minutes later, Tank pulled his truck into a parking space in front of the diner. The sky had delivered on its promise and it was raining steadily. He watched the river of water run down his windshield as he thought for a moment. He had to play this very carefully. Maeve had been short tempered lately, and he didn't want to piss her off. She was making great strides in her balance and her strength, but emotionally she just wasn't herself. He knew if the shoe were on the other foot, he would be a bear to deal with. He figured she just needed time. He hoped anyhow.

He got out of the truck and hurried to the door to take shelter under the front awning. The sign was moved to closed and the door was locked. He could see her head through the pass-through window where Pete put the orders when they were done. It looked like she was scrubbing down all the stainless-steel surfaces. She looked tired. A wisp had escaped the elastic band that held her long blonde hair back into a ponytail. He wanted to reach over and tuck it behind her ear, then take her in his arms and kiss her. He missed her. He missed intimacy with her. They hadn't moved past him kissing her on her forehead and being there as her best friend. He was afraid they never would.

He waited until she straightened up, then he knocked on the door, pressing his face against the window, making a goofy expression for good measure. After all, how can you be mad at a man when he's acting silly?

A quick cloud passed over her face, *was she angry,* before she smiled and waved at him, giving him the 'wait a second' finger.

He put his hands on his hips in mock exasperation and impatience and waited for her to make her way to him and open the door.

"Pete call you?" she asked, the pissed look returning to her eyes.

"Can't a guy ask a girl to get pizza with him?" he said looking hurt and avoiding the question.

"Not if he's going to be a pain in the ass beforehand."

"I won't be," he promised. "Whatcha doing and when will you be done?" He hoped she would decide he stopped by chance, but he wouldn't lie to her or insult her by asking where Pete was.

"I have to finish up before I go. I assume we're getting Harbor New York."

"Is there another place to get pizza?" he asked.

"Yeah, no," she agreed.

"So, what can I do to help?" He looked at her steadily, letting her know he knew she could do it, but he would have helped her before the accident so this shouldn't be any different.

"You don't have to," she said, waiting for him to screw up.

"Of course not, but I always helped when I stopped by any other time before you had finished the close."

"True," she agreed. "Okay, if you can bring that dish rack of glasses over here for me, I can put them away. The last thing that needs done is the coffee maker needs the vinegar run through it."

He smiled at her, happy that she didn't fight him and that they would be working together like before. He lifted the heavy rack of glasses and moved them to the stainless-steel counter so Maeve could put them on the shelves above, and he filled the coffee maker with the vinegar mixture and pressed the button. As he turned to check on Maeve, he heard her swear.

"Shit!" Then the sound of breaking glass shattered the quiet.

"Maeve, you okay?" Tank moved toward her as he watched her seem to shrink. She began to shake violently, her eyes wide and vacant. Her mouth was gaped open as she gasped for air.

He didn't know if he should touch her. He ached to hold her, but something warned him to stay back. *Shit*. He ignored his instinct. He reached for her, but she slapped his hand away. Stunned, he watched her as she tried to run, but her leg betrayed her.

He reached for her again, but she just kept pulling away from him, trying to walk, her crutches swinging on her arms like grotesque tentacles with a mind of their own.

"Maeve, honey, breathe."

"I can't," she yelled at him. "I can't."

She was sobbing now, looking for an out, her head swiveling back and forth in sheer panic. She wanted out of the restaurant, away from Tank and everything he represented. She straightened her crutches and lurched forward, tugging at the door, trying to escape.

He followed her.

"Maeve," he said as softly as he could, hoping she could hear him. She struggled her way down the street, the rain plastering her hair to her head. She didn't even seem to notice. His heart was in his throat, waiting for the crutches to slide on the slippery wet sidewalks.

The rain came down in sheets. Because of that there was no one out to witness Maeve's struggle. He would be eternally grateful for that. She was out of her mind, not thinking. He couldn't believe she had flipped that quickly. Just because a glass fell and broke.

He remembered the sound, a loud shattering in the quiet diner. Breaking glass.

Her accident.

Probably the last thing she heard was the sound of the crash and breaking glass.

He had fallen in beside her, talking to her as she kept up her determined march in the rain, her prosthetic leg starting to drag behind, her arms supporting most of the weight.

"Maeve, honey. It's okay. I'm here. Breathe, sweetie. Breathe." He swiped his forearm across his face not sure if he was wiping rain or tears from his eyes. She just kept going, but he could tell she was getting tired.

Suddenly, she turned at the wooden sidewalk ramp that led to the beach.

No, he thought. *That wood is slippery.* He put a hand on her arm, but she angrily shook it off.

She moved down the ramp toward the beach, the ocean drawing her like a savior.

"Maeve, sweetie. We need to get you help." He regretted having to say it, but it needed to be said.

She tried to whirl around, to confront him, but she slipped, her good leg leaving her. She grasped the handrails in desperation to stop herself from falling, her crutches hanging helplessly from her arms. Tank rushed to her and lifted her in his arms, crushing her to him, whispering he was sorry, begging her to come back to him.

She fought him with everything she had. She twisted and turned in his arms like a wild woman, and he held on for the ride. She hit him, pounding her fists into his chest, his shoulders, his arms.

He took it stoically, the whole time telling her he had her.

She screamed at him to leave her.

"Never," he said, holding her even tighter as her fists continued to find places to land their anger.

"Just fucking leave me. I'm not whole. I'm broken. Just leave me, please, just go." The words ended in a sob.

"I will never leave you again, Maeve. I promise. I'm sorry I let you down before and let you walk away. I'll never do it again. I'm so sorry, honey," he told her as the rain poured down on them, washing their faces, their tears. "I thought I wasn't good enough for you. I just wasn't good enough," he cried as he kissed her eyes, her cheeks.

She pulled back like she had been struck. His heart tore apart.

"So, now that I'm damaged, you're good enough?" She spat the words at him, her eyes blazing with anger.

"No, honey. I finally realized I was. I really was good enough for you the whole time."

*I*nstead of taking her back up the ramp and out of the rain, Tank carried her to the ocean's edge. The waves were pounding, keeping time with the storm. He carried her into the surf as the elements beat on them, the heavens washing away the pain.

He held her as she sobbed, frightened and confused, wounded and broken in pieces. The waves hit them, rocked them, punished them, cleaned them, and they stayed there. Tank holding her until she finally stopped sobbing and stared at the horizon, watching the waves pull back out into the boiling sea.

"Put me down," she asked. Not a defiant demand.

"The waves are strong, honey."

"I know," she told him. "I want to feel them."

He wasn't sure if it was the right thing to do for her leg, but he knew it was the right thing to do for her soul, so he gently set her down, both arms wrapped around her, keeping her safe.

He felt the ocean pulling her trying to claim her, and he smiled as she planted the crutches firmly on each side of her body. He watched her slowly come back to him. His Maeve. But she was different. She looked defeated.

"I'm tired, Tank," she said, still not looking at him.

"I know, honey," he told her, his arms locked around her body.

"I think I need to talk to someone. I think I need some help."

"I'll help you do that. I'll stay by your side and help you do that. Can I do that for you? Can I come back and stay by your side?"

"Yes," she said, turning her face to his. "Yes," she repeated as she lay her head on his shoulder, finally home where she belonged.

26

The rain had stopped. Tank and Maeve sat on the couch in her living room. Tank had built a small fire in the fireplace to take the chill out of the air. Maeve let him towel dry her hair and helped her change into a pair of sweats and an oversized sweatshirt. He tucked her into a soft throw and went into the bathroom to strip down to his boxers, hanging his wet clothes over the shower rod. When he came back, he was surprised to see her smiling until he realized he was wearing his boxer shorts that proclaimed the word shrimp should only be used to describe seafood.

"I need to make a phone call, Maeve," he told her as he drew her into his arms. She rested her head against his chest, breathing in his salty scent.

"I know," she said.

"Do you want me to do it here, or do you not want to listen?"

"No. I'm okay. Do it here."

He kissed her lips, briefly, chastely. He had no intention of starting or finishing anything like that tonight. She smiled again, tired pain etched in her face.

"Hello, Jaxx. It's Tank. Are you busy? Can you and Betty come over to Maeve's house? Oh, and stop by my house on the way and grab me some clothes while you're at it."

Jaxx didn't questions. He kissed his wife and child goodbye for the evening and he and Betty went to help a friend.

When Jaxx arrived, Tank had just finished combing the tangles out of Maeve's hair. He kissed her when he left her on the couch to let Jaxx in. Instantly, Betty was by Maeve's side. Maeve reached out a hand and pulled gently on her soft ears, marveling at the wisdom in the giant dog's eyes.

"Hey, Maeve," Jaxx said as he came up to the couch and sat on the floor making himself eye level with her.

"Hi, Jaxx." Her eyes looked swollen and wounded.

"I think you had a bad night tonight, huh?" Jaxx asked, talking to her in his soothing voice, using his eyes to calm her, winning her trust. Tank leaned back against the wall, watching the exchange. He wanted to stay out of the way, but he was ready to be by her side in an instant.

"Yeah. I kinda flaked." She smiled wanly. "Imagine that. I was always the steady one."

"Yeah, me, too." He appeased her, wondering if she was really ready. If she had finally surrendered to the knowledge that she couldn't do it alone.

"Jaxx, I need help."

"Yes, honey, you do."

"Can you help me call your friend?"

"I have his card right here for you. Do you want me to call him? I have his emergency number."

"Is it okay to do that?"

"It's okay." Jaxx pulled his phone out of his pocket and entered the number he knew by heart. After a few seconds, he was talking quietly to the man on the other end of the phone. Then he held the phone out to Maeve.

"Hi...I'm...um...I'm Maeve."

*J*axx stayed until he was certain Maeve was comfortable. She still seemed a little shell shocked, and he know that it could take days, even weeks to shake the aftermath of a PTSD episode like Tank had described to him. Jaxx was certain his therapist could help, would help, he just wasn't completely convinced that Maeve had made the commitment. *You're not being fair,* he reminded himself. *She has just gone through hell. Give her time.* He was just so worried about her and he didn't want her to back out, for her sake and for Tank's.

It was midnight when he and Betty left them. Tank lifted Maeve and put her in the shower chair, letting the warm water flow over her body, for the second time water soothing her soul. Using a soft sponge he washed her, carefully examining her stump, looking for damage. It looked red and a little raw in one spot. He would have the watch if for infection, but other than a few bruises, she looked okay. It shocked him, the amount of weight she had lost, her rib bones showing against her skin. He soaped her carefully as she closed her eyes and tilted her head back, letting the water envelop her. When he was done cleaning her, he stepped in with her, quickly washing away the residue from the saltwater. He was out of the shower in a minute and dried off. He pulled a clean fluffy towel off the shelf and wrapped Maeve in it, easily picking her up out of the chair. He carried her into her bedroom and lay her down on her bed, pulling the covers over her, nesting her in a cocoon.

In a minute, the lights were out and he had slid in with her, pulling her over to him, putting her head on his shoulder. She sighed and snuggled closer, gathering his warmth.

"Are you cold?" he asked, kissing the top of her still damp hair.

"A little," she admitted. He turned to his side and wrapped both arms around her pulling her tight against his chest.

He lay there listening to her breathe, feeling the tension slowly leave her body. It had been so long since she lay in his arms like this. He missed it. He missed her, and he was afraid he wouldn't ever get his Maeve back. He didn't care about her leg, the jagged scar across her cheek or the shiny disc scar where the turn signal had pierced her skin. Her body wasn't Maeve. He was glad her smile was still the same. Her smile could light up the world. Suddenly he found himself smiling in the darkness, memories of that beautiful, radiant smile watching him as he worked with her brother on Jennifer's childhood home. She was always proud of him. Of his strength and toughness, but she also knew his kind and generous side, and she was proud of that, too. She had told him that often. He just never believed her. He never believed that Maeve didn't deserve better than him. He wouldn't trap her so that she was free to be with the very best man that she could have. He knew know that he was an idiot. His friends had told him that a million times. He should have listened. Maeve's breathing was light and steady. She was asleep in his arms where she belonged.

*H*e woke with a start. Something wasn't right. He tried to clear his head, to remember where he was when he realized a soft hand was stroking his chest. He dipped his head and kissed the top of Maeve's head, her hair dry and sweet smelling.

"I've always loved the way your muscles form your chest. You always made me feel safe." He stroked his fingers lightly down her upper arm, soothing her. She tilted her face and nipped at his chin.

She needed to stop doing that.

He put his hand on the back of her neck and pulled her in, nestling her face in the crook of his chin, willing her to go back to sleep.

Instead she kissed his earlobe.

She knew damn well what happened when she kissed his earlobe.

That's what happens, he thought struggling to ignore what was happening in his groin.

Maeve did not ignore it. She celebrated it, her touch firm and commanding.

Stop it. He ground his teeth.

She reached her hands up to his face and cupped them around his cheeks, drawing his lips to hers. She kissed him, forcing his mouth open with her tongue. Maeve had always been an aggressive partner, sharing equally in the instigation.

It was too soon. *I could hurt her.* The thought deflating the mood. She fixed that situation and kissed him deeper, parting her lips, inviting him to enter her mouth, to explore the places he had known so well but had been missing from.

She rolled him on top of her and wrapped her arms around him, celebrating his strength, his muscle bulk. She missed the feeling of a solid man. She felt him stiffen. She knew he was afraid of hurting her, but she felt confident. She knew she wanted him and not because she was scared and angry and hurt, but because she loved him. She had always loved him. And she had hurt him. She knew she could never take that back, but she could try to make it right. First, by making love to the man she adored, and second, by working hard to get well.

She turned her attention to the first task.

27

"Hey, sis." Ryker stood up and embraced Maeve, giving her a swift peck on the cheek. He was happy to see her face full and radiant, the haunted shadows gone from her eyes. "Good evening, Beau," he said as he scratched the beautiful golden retriever behind the ears.

"He says you can do that all night." She smiled down at the dog by her side. Beau looked into his master's eyes and was happy with what he saw there. His tail wagged, pleased with himself.

Tank walked on the other side of Maeve holding her hand as she made her way to the fire pit without her arm crutches. It had been a long struggle, always two steps forward, three steps back. But they did it together. The three of them, and if he had anything to say about it, there would soon be four of them. Maeve was still apprehensive about becoming a mommy, her confidence not at that level yet, but he knew, in time she would get there. She had come so far.

He had moved in with her, driving her to the diner every morning before work and helping her finish up there in the evening when he was done with his shift with Ryker. Beau never left her side except when he was exiled to her office when she was in the kitchen of the diner, but he was never far from her, always ready to calm her stress or steady her body.

He was trained to recognize when she was losing control, or her stress level started to rise. He was also trained to steady her and help her if she lost her balance. If Maeve wanted, she could even tell Beau to flip the wall switch to turn on a light or retrieve a dropped pen. Sometimes Maeve let Beau do it even if she didn't need it because it made him so happy to help her. In the evening, they often met Maddy and Jaxx so Beau and Betty could run along the beach, Belle toddling behind, trying to keep up with her best buddies.

Maeve settled into a camp chair close to the fire. The evenings were chilly now and the big bonfire was welcome. Jennifer slipped a mug of steaming hot chocolate into Maeve's hand.

"Frangelico?" Maeve asked.

"Is there any other way?" Jennifer replied as she picked up her own mug and held it up. "The last time we were all gathered around our fire pit, I got engaged and we started a new chapter. A lot has happened since then, some good, some bad, but the best part is the fact that we are all friends. We hold each other up. We're there for each other. To us, best of friends, forever and always."

The girls raised their cocoa mugs, the guys their beer. It was quiet. Everyone content to gaze into the fire. Jennifer spoke again.

"I never wanted to come back to Grey's Harbor. I really never wanted to see you guys again. I didn't realize how much I missed, what I would have missed if I hadn't come home."

"I didn't grow up here, but I am definitely home," Jaxx said in a rare moment of sentiment. Ryker and Bridger groaned, and Tank punched him lightly in the shoulder.

"Don't get weak on me brother," Tank told him, handing him another beer. Then he made his way back to Maeve, back to where he belonged.

WOULD YOU LIKE TO SAMPLE SOME MORE OF LARK'S STORIES?

Turn the page for a sneak peek of Teardrops and Flip Flops - A Gone to the Dog's Camper Romance

Teardrops and Flip Flops

LARK GRIFFING

CHAPTER 1

*R*uby chewed on the end of her pen, concentrating on her newest list. Retirement. George looked over and noticed her scowl. He studied her for a moment, and his heart swelled with love. This woman, his woman, he loved her the moment he set eyes on her so many years ago. She was fiery and stubborn, and full of adventure. So different from him. He remembered the first time he saw her. She stood on the top of a bale of straw, her hands on her hips, her auburn hair shining copper in the sun. She was barking orders to two young men, telling them where to move the other bales in order to set the stage for the photographs of the children. Ruby was in charge, and she would be damned if it wasn't going to be perfect. He jumped in and followed her every direction. She leaned on him, and he made things happen. Everything fell into place from there.

That was their senior year in college. They dated for six months, he proposed, she said yes, and that was that. He always knew she was just comfortable with him. He suspected she loved him but wasn't in love with him. George was sorry she missed that in her life, but he had it, and he loved every day of it.

She scowled again and jotted something else on her list; a sea green three by five card charged with keeping her world in order. She had a stack of them next to her chair, color coded, regulated to different aspects of her life. Her life, not what she expected, he knew that. She yearned for adventure; he yearned for family. Neither of them got their wish. All her dreams of adventure buried under her work load, and his dreams of children, dashed by infertility.

"Why are you scowling? What is it that makes that pretty face of yours look sad?"

"I was just thinking."

"That's what I was afraid of. You thinking often equals me working." He smiled at her indulgently, remembering the brick walkway she was 'just thinking about' one day that took him three weekends and then a call to a landscaper to finish. He just wasn't the handy type.

"I was thinking about when we retire. What we can do."

"We can do anything we want. Just name it. I am at your service." He figured she would want to get a condo somewhere on a beach or maybe cruise around Panama. That wasn't his idea of a good time. He was a homebody and would rather stay in his easy chair and watch the most recent loss of his favorite Cleveland sports team.

"I want to buy a trailer and travel the country, living like gypsies. Wouldn't that be awesome?" Ruby turned and looked at him, her eyebrows raised in excitement, her beautiful green eyes flashing with a quest for adventure.

George groaned inwardly. Here we go again, he thought. Five years ago, it was the Appalachian Trail. Two years ago, it was the Camino de Santiago. She dreamed, she read, she watched videos. Of course, it didn't happen. It never did. Time didn't allow such dalliances. At least this time, it didn't involve walking hundreds, perhaps thousands of miles. He smiled brightly at her and made a noncommittal guttural noise.

Ruby sighed. She knew that sound. That was George's way of humoring her without starting an argument. She knew he would never go for her idea. Sure, he would placate her, maybe even go to an RV show with her to feed her dream, but deep inside he would hope for her to move on to the next idea, the next imagined adventure. If he waited long enough, she would. He thought it was because she eventually lost interest in the idea. The truth was, she just gave up. She knew when things were hopeless. She had learned that during her early years, those tender, formative years of childhood. That part of her was bottled up tightly, never to see the light of day. George just figured she was flighty, moving from one set of dreams to another. What he didn't know was she figured out a long time ago when to cut her losses.

Ruby chewed her pen some more and added to the list: Assateague Island, Mount Washington, Newfound Gap, Canyon of the Ancients... all the places she had dreamed of seeing or had read about when she was a kid, using her imagination to escape the special kind of horror that only she knew.

George understood when he had to make an accommodating move. He put down his newspaper and peered over his cheaters.

"So, what's on your list? Different kinds of travel trailer things?" he asked, trying hard to feign interest. He knew better though. She knew him inside and out. There was no fooling her. "Okay, seriously, I could think about it. What, you want to be like those people we saw on the TV the other night, the ones who sold everything and lived in their motor home?"

"No," Ruby laughed at the thought of George leaving his beloved chair and giant TV to travel in a house on wheels. "I couldn't torture you that much. I was thinking more like traveling a few weeks at a time, seeing the country, and then coming home so you could, you know, decompress, or something." She smiled, encouraging him to warm to the idea. "But, there are so many places I want to see. I mean, I love the vacations we've taken. The Caribbean cruise was very nice, and D.C. in spring, with all those cherry blossoms were beautiful, but traveling the open road, going wherever we want, whenever we want would be amazing." With that, Ruby scribbled two more places on her mint green index card; Juneau, Alaska and Banff, Canada.

"I think that sounds ... interesting, dear," said George with as much enthusiasm as he could muster. "You work on your ideas and let me know what you think. I'm going to take a shower and turn in early. It was a hard day at the office today, and I'm feeling tired." George rose and tenderly kissed his wife of twenty-four years on the top of the head. Her hair was silky and warm. "We've got time to plan. We won't be retiring any time soon," sighed George as he contemplated the next nineteen years of working at the accounting firm. Most people would find that idea frightening, Ruby certainly would, but he found comfort in the routine. Order was his mantra.

He climbed the stairs thinking he felt so tired that night. Not good. Not good at all. As he turned the corner, he looked one last time lovingly at his wife, his angel. It was okay that she didn't love him with the passion that he felt for her. He just felt lucky to have her in his life. But a travel trailer? The thought pained him.

CHAPTER 2

*R*uby had a hard time concentrating. She was editing an article about the horror of tan lines, and she just wasn't feeling it. Usually she enjoyed the weird things she learned when she edited. The company she worked for provided writing and editing services, and she worked on everything from textbooks to magazine articles. Not only did her job provide her with a living wage, but Ruby was now an expert on the proper way of rolling on a condom with panache, making the perfect Mojito, and historic myths about our founding fathers that don't hold water. Overall, the condom article was one of her favorites, although obtaining semen from a prize race horse for artificial insemination was a close second.

Despite the fascinating tan line dilemma, Ruby's thoughts kept wandering to life on the road in a camper. It had been three weeks since she had first broached the subject to George. Once, over a particularly fine meal of Beef Wellington at the Greenland Tavern, she tried again, regaling him with information about trailers that sported recliners and an outdoor TV. George tried to be enthusiastic, but the Wellington had left his stomach queasy, and he had spent the evening popping Tums.

The ringing of her phone interrupted her musing, and she reached absently for it.

"Hello. This is Ruby, how may I help you?"

"Ruby, it's Tom. I'm sorry…"

"Tom? Why are you calling me? What's going on?" There was an awkward silence. The sound of a clearing throat. "Is something wrong with George? Oh God, Tom. What happened?"

"Ruby, you have to get to General right away. They've taken him by ambulance. I think it's his heart. I'm so sorry, Ruby. If there is anything I can do… anything the firm can do. Please let me know."

*uby burst through the elevator doors, looking around wildly for anyone to help her. A woman in blue scrubs covered with happy, puppy dog faces cupped Ruby's elbow with her hand and gently guided her to a reception desk.

"My husband. I'm trying to find my husband. They said this floor. I think, his heart."

"What's your name, honey?" asked the woman behind the desk with the expansive bosom and warm, calming smile. "And what is your husband's name?"

"George, his name is George. George Dunning. I'm Ruby. His wife. Ruby." Her hands flew to her hair, trying to pat down the flyaways, vaguely aware she might be disheveled.

"Ah, here he is, George Dunning. They are getting him ready for surgery right now. I have some paperwork for you." The woman with the comforting soft curves glanced behind Ruby, catching the slight shake of the head from the dog scrub lady. Ruby caught the exchange.

"Wait. What? What's wrong? Surgery?"

The cheerful puppy once again took Ruby's elbow and led her down the hall. She began to speak in a quiet comforting voice.

"Your husband has had heart issues. He is being prepped for surgery. I don't know if I can get a doctor to speak with you just now, they are getting prepared, but I will see what I can do." She guided

Ruby to a hard, orange plastic chair situated by a glossy, wide leaf plant and a contemporary painting of an angel, or maybe a flock of birds, it was hard to tell.

A set of double doors burst open and a gurney rumbled toward them at a quick pace. Ruby followed puppy scrub's gaze and realized her George was on that gurney. She jumped up from the chair and ran to his side. The gurney didn't stop.

"George. I love you, George. You're going to be okay. You have to be okay." She was running to keep up. George reached his hand toward hers and smiled a tired smile at her worried face.

"Don't worry, sweetheart. I've had the happiest years of my life with you. It's all good."

"Don't talk like that, George. The doctors will fix it. I promise. I know they will."

"Hush, Ruby. Listen. I want you to be happy. I want you to always be happy. Promise me that."

"I am happy. George you make me happy. I love you."

"I know you, Ruby. I know your heart. Get my things from my desk at work..."

"Excuse me," interrupted an efficient looking doctor with the most startling blue, cold eyes. "I need to get this man into my operating room."

"This man is my husband, and I love him, and I want to know what is going on."

"If I stop to explain this all to you, he won't be around to love."

Ruby gasped in surprise, not expecting the brusque manner or the cold, hard reality of his words.

"Ruby, I love you. I think this is my last stop. I bought you a..." and with that George's eyes closed, and the medical crew whisked him away. Puppy scrubs grabbed Ruby and barred her from following them.

PURCHASE TEARDROPS AND FLIP FLOPS

From Amazon
or
Click the linked cover below

SIGN UP FOR LARK'S NEWSLETTER

Would you like to know when Lark releases her next book? Do you want a sneak peek at sample chapters? If so, sign up for Lark Griffing's newsletter.

Subscribe now

Or use this URL to subscribe

http://eepurl.com/dH1mzz

ACKNOWLEDGMENTS

As always, the creative writing of a novel is only the beginning. There are so many other things that go into creating a plausible story. For one thing, it needs to be believable. I want to thank Chardon Fire Captain John Blaugh, EMS Instructor, for answering all my medical questions. It was incredibly helpful. If there are any medical errors in my writing, it's because I took liberties and not because John gave me bad advice. After all, I write fiction. I get to make stuff up, right?

Of course my editor, JC Wing, and my readers are always there for me. Without them, my writing would be a mess. A special shout out to my sister-in-law, Tracy Simiele, who always enthusiastically reads my stories and gives thoughtful, intelligent feedback. Thanks, sis.

The last person to thank is my soulmate, my husband, Joe. God could not have given me a better person to spend my life with. He gets me. For that I am eternally grateful.

ABOUT THE AUTHOR

Lark Griffing is all about stories of adventure and romance. Whether writing about a recent Widowed women discovering life in a teardrop trailer or a teenage girl dealing with evil spirits in her aunt's ancient house on the cliffs above the sea, Lark sets the story in motion and the reader is never really sure where or how it's going to end. Often that reader gets a surprise they weren't expecting, and Lark likes that.

Lark Griffing is a dabbler. Her hobbies are many and varied, from SCUBA diving to backpacking, kayaking to knitting. You never know what you're going to get on any given day if you hang with her.

Her husband and boys are used to her running off in all directions, and they humor her because they know that with Lark, an adventure awaits them. The only members of her family who are not up for the fun are her tabby cat, Dickens and her golden doodle, Maggie. The two of them would prefer staying curled up together holding down the fort until Lark comes bursting back through the door.

Keep up with Lark at her website:

www.LarkGriffing.com

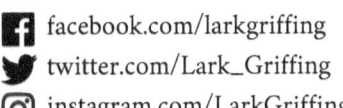

facebook.com/larkgriffing
twitter.com/Lark_Griffing
instagram.com/LarkGriffing

ALSO BY LARK GRIFFING

Grey's Harbor Stories

GREY'S LANDING

GREY'S HARBOR with various authors

HOPE ADRIFT

Gone To the Dogs Camper Romance Series

TEARDROPS AND FLIP FLOPS

TEARDROPS AND REST STOPS

Young adult novels:

THE LAST TIME I CHECKED I WAS STILL HERE

THE STARFISH TALISMAN

Short Story Collections

DOG ON THE DOORSTEP

www.ingramcontent.com/pod-product-compliance
Lightning Source LLC
Chambersburg PA
CBHW051253250626
47155CB00009B/3281